My name is Callum Ormond.
I am fifteen
and I am a hunted fugitive . . .

Elliot

CONSPIRACY 365

BOOK SEVEN: JULY

GABRIELLE LORD

Hodder
Children's
Books

A division of Hachette Children's Books

Note: This story is set in Australia, where July is a winter month

First published by Scholastic Australia Pty Ltd in 2010
First published in Great Britain in 2010 by Hodder Children's Books,
under licence from Scholastic Australia Pty Ltd

A Catalogue record for this book is available from the British
Library

ISBN 978 0 340 99650 8

Printed and bound by Bookmarque Ltd, Croydon, Surrey

The paper and board used in this paperback by Hodder Children's
Books are natural recyclable products made from wood grown in
sustainable forests. The manufacturing processes conform to the
environmental regulations of the country of origin.

Hodder Children's Books
A division of Hachette Children's Books
338 Euston Road, London NW1 3BH
An Hachette UK company
www.hachette.co.uk

To Amber, Cal, Holly, Jimmy and Matt

PREVIOUSLY ...

1 JUNE
I run away from the wreckage of the Ormond Orca, just as it explodes. I dodge my pursuers in the forest and make it to the town of Big River, where I hide in an empty scout hall.

5 JUNE
Finally back in the city, I dream about my dead great-uncle. He assures me I'll find the answers I need. I hope he's right.

19 JUNE
My mate Boges sets me up in a mansion and tells me he's found a guy who'll give us the gangster Sligo's new address for four hundred bucks.

20 JUNE
I am convinced Sligo has the Ormond Jewel, so I need money. I call Griff Kirby, who said he could help me earn quick cash. The work on offer ends up being a carjacking. I get myself beaten up while trying to stop it.

24 JUNE

Boges scores Sligo's address, so I go to Repro's to convince him to help me break into the safe and retrieve the Jewel. He thinks the job's too dangerous.

25 JUNE

Winter offers to help us get inside Sligo's place, which prompts me to try again for Repro's help.

29 JUNE

It's a race against time as Repro battles to find the correct combination to Sligo's safe. Finally, he cracks the code and the door swings open to reveal the Ormond Jewel! I also spot a photo of Winter wearing it! Sligo returns and we speed away in a gardening truck. We're chased to the edge of a cliff and forced out on foot. Repro disappears into the scrub, while I make use of an abandoned hang-glider and take off into the sky.

Walking back to the city, cops pull me up and drag me in for questioning. They think I'm Ben Galloway, but I know that false ID won't hold up for long.

30 JUNE

The cops want to transfer me to another station, but I intercept their keys and take off in a squad car. A high-speed chase leads all the way down to the sea. On foot, I run down a jetty, jump onto a jet ski and ride away. A fishing boat appears from nowhere, sending me crashing into the water. I'm entangled in a fishing net, trapped underwater . . .

1 JULY

184 days to go . . .

12:00 am

Tonnes of water swirled all around me as I struggled and floundered, trying to claw my way out of the enclosing fishing net. I knew I couldn't hold my breath much longer. My lungs were desperate for air, and already I could feel my mouth wanting to open, even though I knew that would be a fatal move. The net tightened, crushing me against the trapped fish. Fins and prickly scales scored my face and hands like tiny razors.

I struggled, panicked and frantic, feeling like my lungs were going to explode. *Pull it up!* I begged the fishing boat silently. *Please pull the net up! Don't let me drown down here!*

The pressure was unbearable. A ringing in my ears built into a crushing surge. My panic escalated. *This is it!*

The pressure shifted as a sudden lurching, swinging motion moved us through the water. The net was lifting! If I could just hold on a few seconds longer! But my lungs suddenly convulsed out of my control, and I gulped . . . air! Wonderful, life-saving air!

The net had broken through the surface of the dark sea, and a huge inhalation of oxygen rushed down my throat. I could breathe—just! Higher and higher the bulging net swung above the water, compressing my body even more with the weight of the huge catch surrounding me. Fish seethed, scraped and hopelessly flailed, pressed against my skin.

12:04 am

The bottom of the net abruptly opened, giving way like the wet explosion of a burst water balloon. I was sent free-falling from about three metres, and dumped on the deck of the boat. The catch skidded out everywhere and I landed with a thud, flat on my back. I was stunned and still struggling for air as fish flapped desperately around me. My breath came in great sobbing gulps. I couldn't do anything except suck in oxygen. I had survived, and that was all I knew or cared about just then.

I pulled a small bream from my face, shook off strings of slimy seaweed from my hair, and spat sea water from my salty lips. The dim glow of the boat's spotlights showed that my hands were bleeding from the tiny incisions made by hundreds of fins and spikes.

'Hey! We've caught ourselves a mermaid!' said a voice nearby. 'Hey skipper! Look what we picked up!'

Wet, black rubber boots stepped up close to my face. I strained my eyes, blinking under the torchlight that was suddenly on me. A young guy was bending over me, his sunburnt face peering out through thick, curly hair. He kicked me gently, like he was checking I was alive.

'Jeez, she's not the prettiest one I've ever seen!' he said to another guy coming up behind him. 'You're pretty badly cut, kid,' he said to me. 'How did you get yourself into this mess?'

A booming voice from a megaphone broke through my consciousness, the words loud and clear. 'Callum Ormond! Stop! Police!'

I struggled to get up. The silhouette of the second deckhand was turned away from me, watching the approaching police boat, *Stingray*.

I looked around for a way out—a way of sneaking off the boat unnoticed. I checked for my backpack. It was still on my shoulders. I still had the Ormond Jewel, but had everything survived being underwater? There was no time to check. A brilliant light was sweeping the surface of the sea nearby, every second getting closer to the deck of the boat that I had landed on. I had to get away or hide! *Think, Cal, think*, shouted the voice in my mind.

'Hey kid, you in trouble?' asked the curly-haired deckhand, squatting down beside me.

'Chuck him over the side!' said the second deckhand, as he backed away from the approaching searchers. He stopped, hands on his hips, shaking his head. 'We don't want any trouble. We don't want cops nosing around here.'

I sure didn't want the cops nosing around either! I scrambled to my feet, almost losing my footing as I skidded in squid ink.

'None of us can afford that,' the second deckhand continued. 'Everyone we've got on board is on the run from something or someone!'

His voice seemed familiar, but before I could think any more about it, the skipper—an old guy with a beard and a black beanie pulled down around his face—appeared. He looked around, confused by all the unexpected commotion surrounding his boat.

'What's going on here?' he demanded, in a thick Greek accent. 'What's with the police? What's with the kid?' he asked, pointing at me, before being interrupted by the megaphone threats from the police boat, which was coming closer every second. The searchlight pierced through the darkness, revealing the choppy surface of the surrounding sea, and the upturned jet ski, bobbing just a few metres away. The threats stopped for a moment, and the skipper stared down at me once more.

'Where the in the world did *you* come from, boy?'

My teeth chattered as I spat more water from my mouth. 'I fell off my jet ski and got tangled up in your fishing net,' I gasped to the skipper towering over me. 'I'm being chased by the police, but I can't let them catch me! I haven't done anything wrong, I swear!'

The police boat was pulling up alongside us now—the voices of the cops shouted above the noise of the engine. They were going to get me. What was I going to do to protect all my stuff? The drawings, the Riddle, the Jewel?

The skipper swung round, yelling at his deck-hands. 'OK you two! What am I paying you for? Don't just stand there! Start sorting the catch!'

I finally hauled myself up, grabbing onto the sides of the fishing boat, thinking I'd have to jump overboard and take my chances in the darkness of the sea.

'So, you're on the run,' barked the skipper.

I was afraid to speak again. I guessed what was going to happen next—he'd call out to the police, and I'd be handed in. Would I be in prison when I got to my sixteenth birthday?

I could hear the police alongside us, preparing to board. The slapping sound of the water against the boat grew stronger, blending with the gaping gills and flapping fish that still encircled me.

What was I going to do? I was so distracted, I barely heard the skipper when he spoke again.

'So, you're on the run,' he repeated. 'Big deal. All of my deckhands are on the run. They're all crooks!'

'Callum Ormond!' roared the loudhailer. 'Reveal your location! Hand yourself in!'

'You'd better get out of sight, fast!' hissed the Greek skipper, before dragging me to the cabin entrance and shoving me down it.

12:14 am

I tumbled into darkness, and crouched quietly, straining to listen to what was happening on deck.

'Seen a kid around here?' demanded the officer's voice from the police boat. 'Fifteen to sixteen years of age? He must have come past here, around the point—he was on a jet ski. There it is, drifting over there, so he has to be around here somewhere.'

Please, I begged the skipper. *Don't change*

your mind and hand me over!

'Haven't seen anyone like that,' the skipper's distinct voice called back. 'Didn't see anyone on a jet ski. Maybe he went that way.'

He covered for me! In the cramped cabin below, my limbs went weak with relief.

But my relief didn't last long.

'We're coming aboard,' the officer continued, dismissively. 'We need to take a look around.'

'You've got no right to board my boat.'

'Hiding something, are you?'

12:19 am

While the argument continued above me, I tried to spot a place to hide. But in a few moments, I'd felt out all there was: four narrow bunk beds, strewn with clothes; two small cupboards; a toilet and shower, and, through a doorway, a tiny kitchen. Other than that, there was a humming fridge that reeked of blood and scales, and a couple of long freezers.

The place was so small, there was nowhere to hide. I couldn't even fit under the bunks. I listened intently through the hatch-opening again.

'OK,' I heard the skipper say. 'I guess I can't stop you from boarding my boat. But I'm not happy about it, officer. We're just trying to do a night's work here. We don't have time to waste.'

Someone thudded down the cabin steps without warning. It was the first deckhand, with the black boots and curly hair. He grabbed me and I thought for a moment he'd been ordered to throw me overboard. I resisted as hard as I could until I realised that he was dragging me towards another hatch, half the size of a normal door, cut low into the wall behind one of the freezers. He jerked the door open and pushed me through the hole. Heat and the stench of diesel fuel slammed me in the face.

'The boss says you gotta get in there!'

I could just make out two large diesel engines in the cramped, gloomy area, but couldn't see anywhere to hide.

'There's some space underneath the diesels— where the mechanic works,' he added, with a shove. 'Get in!'

I crawled deeper into the stinking, black hole. There was just enough room for me and my backpack to squeeze under the engines. Cold and wet, I flattened myself into the space.

The hatch door slammed shut, and the freezer was dragged back into position.

The cops started boarding. I heard their muffled voices, followed by them thudding down the steps into the cabin. There were things being lifted and thrown about, doors opening and

closing. The footsteps came closer and closer . . .
I cowered, hoping they wouldn't find the hatch
I was in.

'Where are the engines?' a voice asked, dash-
ing that hope instantly.

I held my breath as the freezer was shifted
once more, revealing the hatch door and my hiding place. The door opened and a beam of light
shone in. I pressed myself against the floor, as
the light played over the diesel engines that I
hoped would obscure me.

A sudden gush of heat rushed out.

'Nothing here except the engines,' someone said,
before coughing and swearing. 'Bloody fumes.'

The door slammed shut.

I barely breathed again until I heard the
police disembark, and *Stingray* sped away to
continue the search for me elsewhere.

1:06 am

Cramped and sweating, I kicked a leg out at the
hatch door—I'd waited long enough for the cops
to move on—I needed to get out. But it wouldn't
budge. I kicked again, this time harder. Still
nothing. They'd locked me in.

4:47 am

Loud thumping woke me up. Despite everything,

I must have slept, or passed out from the fumes.

'You can come out of there now,' said the skipper, opening the door. Soft light fell on my face, and I sucked up the fresh air.

Awkwardly, I squeezed my stiff and stinging body out from under the engines and emerged. The skipper wasn't smiling any more. There were no jokes about his crew all being on the run. His face was stern and hard.

'You must have done something real bad, boy,' he said as I lifted myself up and leaned against the edge of the freezer. 'You owe me.'

'You saved me,' I said. 'But I haven't done anything wrong,' I added. 'I'm innocent.'

'Aren't we all?' he scoffed, sarcastically. 'You work for me now.'

'Work for you? For how long?' I asked.

He shrugged. 'Until you've paid me back. Otherwise I give you to the police. Understand?'

I nodded. I knew I had no option. I'd escaped the net but was still trapped.

'I'll send one of the boys down to get you started. Stay here until then.'

He turned and vanished up the narrow steps.

5:03 am

The curly-haired deckhand jumped down the steps into the cabin, his narrowed eyes watching me with curiosity. He didn't seem hostile, but I was very wary of what he was going to tell me to do.

'The Little Mer-*boy*,' he joked. 'I'm George,' he said, his face grimacing with dislike at his name, 'but everyone calls me Squid.' He pulled a duffel bag down from a luggage rack. 'We've just pulled in to the fish market wharf.'

'OK,' I said, expectantly.

'So, Merboy, what's your story?'

'The name's *Tom*, actually,' I said, even though the police boat had been hollering out my real name, just hours ago.

He considered this for a moment, before saying, 'Nah, I like Merboy better. What's in the bag?' he asked, nodding towards my backpack.

'Nothing much. What's *your* story?'

'Pretty much the same as the other guys. Most of us take this kind of work because there are no questions asked.'

'But you've just asked me two of them,' I pointed out.

He laughed, dumping the duffel bag on one of the narrow bunks. 'So I did, you're right. And you just avoided answering both. Sounds like you'll fit right in with our crew!' He sat down beside his bag before continuing. 'If you've done this type of work before you'll know that casual deckhands on fishing boats are often on the run from something. Maybe it's the law, maybe it's the missus, and maybe they just want to get lost for a while. Whatever the case, there are a lot of crooks.'

'And you're not one of them?' I asked, smiling.

'Not really. Never done anything really bad.'

'Same,' I said. 'I just need to lie low for a while.' I shrugged. 'Family stuff.'

'Mate, I understand. But all the same, you'll need to stay on your toes. The cops do a lot of lightning raids; they swoop down on the wharf, looking for people who might be trying to avoid them. We're trying to catch fish, and the cops are trying to catch us!'

He stood back up and stuck out his hand with a grin. It was grimy and scaly, but I shook it.

'Welcome aboard, Merboy. Stick with me, keep your eyes peeled and you should be OK. I can show you the ropes.' He frowned for a second, peering closely at me. 'You sure you haven't worked the boats before?'

'Never,' I said, before he backed away, wrinkling his nose in disgust.

'No-one smells good round here, but you smell like the bottom of the bait tin! How 'bout you wash up a bit and I get you some dry gear?' He rummaged through his bag and threw me a black shirt and a pair of work overalls. 'Here.

You can have these.' He pulled a worn towel out of the cupboard and threw that at me as well.

I followed Squid up to the deck and onto the wharf. The skipper and the other deckhand were busy sorting and stacking big plastic tubs of fish.

The skipper looked up briefly as we passed. 'Show him where to go,' he ordered Squid. 'When I've got time, I'll show him how to clean and scale. Meantime, he can be a wheeler with you.'

Squid nodded.

'Wheeler?' I asked, hurrying after him along the wharf.

'After the fish are auctioned,' he explained, 'the wheelers stack and load the boxes onto trolleys and wheel them over to the loading areas where the trucks are waiting.'

We'd reached a tiled shower area, and Squid nodded towards one of the open cubicle doors. I stepped into one and locked the door behind me, then quickly rummaged through my backpack to check how everything had held up. I peeled the tape off the package at the bottom of my bag, and tipped the Ormond Jewel out.

I could hardly believe it. Somehow it had survived, just like me. I stared at it again, amazed at the emerald and precious stones. I turned it over and looked at the images on the back—a red rose and rosebud. Water had dampened the edges of the Riddle and the drawings, but they were OK. I re-wrapped everything tightly and stuck the tape down again, as best I could. My phone wasn't so lucky—it had not survived the drenching. Water streaked across the dead screen.

It was rough standing under the spray of hot water—every little cut on my body stung like crazy. It was so painful, but knowing everything I'd collected was safe got me through. Without realising it, the gruff skipper had given me some serious cover.

'I need to dry my gear out,' I said to Squid as I came out of the shower cubicle.

'Take it back to the *Star. Star of Mykonos*, that's the name of our boat. Find somewhere to hang it. Hurry up!'

'And I need to make a phone call first. Urgently,' I added, showing him the dead screen on my phone.

'It'll cost ya,' he said, reaching into his back pocket.

'How much?'

'Five bucks.'

'Five bucks for one quick call?'

'It's a good deal for an urgent call!'

I was in no position to argue. I dug into a pocket in my backpack, scrounged up five bucks in coins and handed it over. In exchange, Squid passed me his mobile.

I stood there, waiting.

'Oh, I get it,' he said. 'Girlfriend, eh? You only got one minute, OK? It'll be my head on the block if you're caught slacking off.'

I ducked back into the cubicle and closed the door.

Boges picked up the phone so fast, like he was there waiting for it to ring.

'You're not going to believe this!' I blurted out.

'Whose phone are you calling from? The state is in lockdown!' he yelled over me. 'There's a man-hunt going on around the beaches. Where are you?'

'I'm at the fish markets.'

'What?'

'I'll explain later, I don't have much time to talk. We've gotta meet. We have everything now. The Riddle, the Jewel.'

'That's great, but I'm serious, you've got to keep out of sight! Hide, blend in, do whatever it takes, and then we can meet up when everything's cooled down again. I'm stuck here at the moment anyway, trying to get my application together for an internship.'

Squid banged on the door. 'Hurry up! The boss wants to know why we're not working!'

'Gotta go?' Boges asked.

'I'll call you,' I said before hanging up.

'Be back here in five!' Squid shouted at me as I ran past him, head down, on my way back to where the fishing boat was moored.

It didn't look like anyone was on board, so I jumped on and draped my damp gear over some crates on the deck. The wind and sun would dry them out soon, I hoped.

I'd been very lucky. I'd escaped the police— again. But Boges was right, and I already knew the whole state would be looking for me. I hoped Oriana de la Force and Vulkan Sligo didn't have any information on where I was.

What Squid said about the police raids on the wharves had me rattled. This was a good enough place to hide out for a while, but I couldn't stay here too long . . . I wanted to meet up with Boges and see what we could make of cracking the double-key code, now that we had both halves— the Ormond Riddle and the Ormond Jewel. I also wanted to know if he'd had any luck tracking down Great-uncle Bartholomew's sister, Millicent.

I could hear Squid yelling out, so I slung my backpack on and jumped off the boat to join him.

Squid and I hurried over to a spot where hundreds of boxes of fish were piled high. The fish auctions were in full swing and the voices of the auctioneers boomed through the area. Buyers and sellers milled around on the wet and slippery floor.

We worked hard, loading the heavy boxes onto our trolleys as they were purchased, and wheeling them through the crowds to the loading dock. Once there, we'd unload them and help the buyers stack them on the backs of their trucks, or in their vans.

As we were lifting a really heavy box of red fish on top of a couple of boxes of flathead, Squid groaned and wiped sweat from his forehead. 'Gary's supposed to be helping us,' he said.

'You mean the other guy?' I asked. 'The other deckhand?' I'd barely seen him—only heard his voice and I hadn't liked what he'd said.

'That's Gary. He's only been working here a few weeks. He just disappears when there's hard work around. I don't like the guy,' Squid continued. 'I don't trust him. I mean, I know you can hardly trust anyone around here, but I *really* don't trust him. The skipper only keeps him on because it's hard to find deckhands.'

8:20 am

Three hours later, the auction was almost finished and the last of the buyers were leaving with their purchases. Behind us, other workers were hosing down the tiled and cement surfaces, clumping around in bulky gumboots.

'I'm so glad this is almost over,' said Squid, sprawling on the ground near a brick wall. 'I need a break.' He took his phone out of his pocket again and started texting someone.

'I'm going to duck back to the boat, to get my gear,' I told him. 'Back in a minute.'

Star of Mykonos

8:32 am

I snatched up my clothes—they were salty and almost stiff—then jammed them into my backpack. I jumped back onto the wharf, hurrying to rejoin Squid.

The place had almost emptied and Squid had disappeared. I lugged the last two containers of sand shark and leatherjacket into the back of a van and looked around again for him. I couldn't see him anywhere.

Just then, a short guy in overalls—the owner of one of the vans we'd loaded—approached me. 'Will you help me with this load, son?' he asked, pulling off his woollen beanie and wiping his forehead with it. 'If you ride with me to my shop and give me a hand at the other end, I'll give you thirty bucks. Another young bloke was supposed to help me, but he's useless. Didn't even show up.'

There was still no sign of Squid, and thirty bucks sounded good to me.

'Sure,' I said, shaking his hand. I felt bad for taking off without saying anything to Squid, but thought I had to take up the opportunity to get away—I had no idea what the skipper would expect me to do next.

'My shop's just a few blocks away,' the guy explained as we drove away from the markets. 'I injured my wrist, and Gary was supposed to help me with the load at the other end, but he decided not to show up.'

Gary? The guy Squid didn't trust?

8:48 am

A few minutes later, we pulled up in front of Mike's Seafood.

'That's me. I'm Mike,' he said, pointing a bandaged hand in the direction of the shop.

'Tom,' I said, before jumping out and walking to the back of the van. I peered around me, keeping a watch on the street in case of police patrols. Mike opened the doors and I began unloading and stacking his trolley.

I wheeled the first lot of containers through his shop and out to the back where there was a big freezer room. Mike awkwardly unbolted the door and it swung open, releasing an icy cloud. It was so cold and frosty in there—it was like stepping inside an igloo in the middle of Antarctica—so I unloaded as fast as I could, my breath steaming out in front of me.

9:25 am

Finally, I stacked the last load onto the trolley.

'Wheel that load into the freezer room too, and then can you wait for me here in the shop? I need to get some cash out to pay you.' He pointed to an ATM down the street. 'Can't spare any from the till, I'm afraid.'

'Sure.'

Just as I was dragging the last heavy box of fish off the trolley, shivering inside the chilly freezer room, a figure appeared in the doorway, his face half-hidden in a dark hoodie.

'I can help you with that,' he said, with an evil chuckle. It was the second deckhand from the *Star of Mykonos*—Gary. As he grabbed hold of the freezer door, I realised too late why his voice had seemed familiar to me back on the boat. On the hand that held the door were *three* fingers! Before I could say or do anything, Three-O shoved me hard up against the trolley, sending me flying backwards into the depths of the freezer!

'I know exactly who you are, Cal Ormond. Did

you think we were all dumb or something?' he said, spitting at my feet. 'Everyone knows who you are!' I jumped up and braced myself, remembering too well how he'd beaten me up at the carpark. 'There's a massive price on your head, Ormond, and you owe me big time! I could have got a thousand bucks for spotting that car. It's time I cashed in!'

He held up a camera phone, and snapped a picture of me.

I lunged at him, but before I reached him, he stepped back and slammed the freezer door shut. My fists slammed into nothing but metal.

I grabbed the door handle and wrenched it, but it wouldn't open.

'Let me out! Let me out, damn it!' I shouted.

I wrenched the door handle again, but nothing happened. I couldn't get out. I banged and bashed, yelling loudly, realising that Three-O must have recognised me back on the boat, followed me here, and now he was off to tell the police and show them my picture.

And I was locked up in the freezer, just waiting for the cops to come and get me.

'Mike!' I shouted, banging uselessly on the door, thinking surely he'd be back any second. He had to let me out before the police turned up. 'I'm locked in the freezer!'

Already my teeth were chattering. Again, I kicked and bashed and pushed the door, but despite its rusty hinges, it wasn't budging. I swung around to see if there was any other way out, but of course there wasn't.

I grabbed my phone out of desperation, but it was still as dead as the bins of fish that surrounded me. I flung it back into my bag, looking around again for a way out.

Who was going to find me first, Mike or the cops? And how long were they going to take? A thermometer on the wall indicated minus twenty-five degrees Celsius. I didn't know how long I could last.

'Let me out!' I shouted and thrashed my body uselessly against the door. I was going to be a dead fish too if I didn't get out fast. A few minutes had passed already, and panic was starting to fester in the pit of my stomach. I'd have to get out of here or I'd die. Being arrested was better than freezing to death.

My fingers and toes were aching with cold and my nose had gone numb. I backed away from the door and huddled, hugging my knees, trying to warm myself up. The cold was travelling through my body fast, making my arms and legs ache. My ears were throbbing too and the bones in my face were hurting.

I got back up and jumped around, clapping my
arms, trying to keep moving. It was impossible
to warm up and I was starting to really freak
out, like I had that night in Treachery Bay when
the sharks were circling, ready to attack. It
had been Dad's words in my mind that got me
through that ordeal. *Think, Cal. Think.* I was
trying to think, trying to work out a plan of
action, but it was like my brain was starting
to freeze, making it impossible. How do you get
through a locked door? Without being a ghost?

The sight of my fingers made me feel dizzy—
they were dead white, and when I pressed them
together, they felt like pieces of wood, as if they
didn't belong to me. Was this the first stage of
frostbite?

I was still racking my brain for a way to open
the door . . . but came up with nothing. Where
was Repro when I needed him? I pictured him in
his tiny living quarters behind the filing cabinets, surrounded by his piles of lost property
and scavenged bits and pieces. And that reminded me of something . . .

The track detonators!

With my clumsy, frozen fingers, I dragged the
backpack off my shoulders and dug around for the
tin containing the blast caps Repro had given me.

I figured if I could wedge them into the cracks

between the door and its hinges, then slam something against the door to trigger them, there might be a chance for me to blow the whole thing open. And get out.

Aside from the fact that I had no idea whether the tin had stayed airtight, protecting the caps when I'd fallen underwater, I had another problem: it was very tightly sealed and my fingers were numb, barely able to move. Feverishly, I battled with the lid, fumbling like a baby as I attempted to get it open.

The intense cold tried to take me down as I battled to prise the lid up. My feet were starting to feel frozen to the floor, like blocks of dead weight, when at last the lid lifted. I threw it aside, and ripped out the mouldy roll that was still in there. Underneath, four blast caps lay flat in the tin. They were dry. They were intact.

It took me ages to fumble the first two caps into position—one above and one beneath the top hinge. But when I went to do the same with the bottom hinge, I realised it wasn't possible. The door didn't hang straight and there was almost no gap between the lower jamb and the metal of the door. Two caps weren't going to be enough.

'Mike!' I shouted again. What in the world had happened to him? 'Help me out of the freezer! Mike, I'm trapped!'

The police were going to show up any minute, and Three-O would get his reward for my capture. I didn't know what to do.

I'd never felt anything like this kind of extreme cold before. My eyelids seemed to be drying out. I blinked desperately, trying to see as I wedged the other two blast caps under the door, in a last-ditch effort. Worried I might explode them early, I flinched as I shoved and kicked them into position.

Now that they were in place, how was I going to detonate them? And how could I be sure that the pressure of the blast would blow the door outward, off its hinges, and not towards me?

I had to try *something*. I *had* to set off the detonators.

All I had was the trolley I'd wheeled in. I grabbed it with fingers that couldn't feel anything any more, and with what was left of my strength I backed it up and then ran and rammed it as powerfully as I could against the door.

All four detonators exploded simultaneously!

The impact of the collision ripped through my body, and the sound and pressure of the explosion in the confined space blasted me back against the freezer wall. Icy splinters speared into my face.

A rush of adrenaline gave me the energy to

get to my feet and check the door. The top hinges had buckled and the bottom hinges were twisted, but the door was still stuck. Instantly I forced my half-frozen body right back into action, and got behind the trolley again. I ran full pelt at the door once more, bashing it with the weight of my body. I felt it shift and buckle. Yelling like a crazy man, I had my third go at it and this time I crash-tackled the door down, completely off its hinges, sprawling sideways as it collapsed to the floor outside.

10:04 am

There was no sign of anyone—Mike, Three-O or the cops. I hesitated, my body madly readjusting to the change in temperature, but I couldn't worry about the mess I was leaving behind. All I knew was that I had to get out of there fast. I grabbed my backpack and ran.

I stumbled out the door of the shop, lopsided and off-balance like Frankenstein's monster. I was starting to thaw, my skin first, then my muscles, and for a few freaky moments it was like I could feel my moving skeleton, each frosty bone of my body within the tissue that was starting to warm up and soften. A quick glance down the road, in the direction of the ATM, showed Mike shouting at Gary as they stormed up the street together, both of them with their mobile phones out. I shivered, increasing my pace, and turned down another street and out of sight.

The sound of sirens started swarming, and in seconds I could hear cop cars skidding to a halt outside Mike's shop. I didn't waste time looking back, I just ran as fast as I could in the opposite direction, forcing my cold, numb legs to stride out and carry me away. Far away from the cops, and far away from the rotten smell of fish.

2 JULY

183 days to go . . .

S Enid Parade, Crystal Beach

7:22 am

I stirred, woken by a distant noise.

After a moment, I shut my eyes and pulled the thick woollen blanket over me again. I was back at the beachside mansion—the place Boges had given me access to—sleeping on the plush rug. I'd had a good night's sleep, sprawled out on the thick carpet, cocooned in its warmth. As soon as I'd made it back here after my crazy day, I'd taken a long, hot, painful shower. Next I'd dragged an extra blanket out of one of the walk-in closets, draped it around me, and crawled into a ball on the floor. I'd pretty much been in this position ever since.

I hoped Boges wouldn't go crazy at me for breaking the don't-touch rules of staying in the house, but I figured he'd understand once he knew I'd almost frozen to death.

The gentle sound of the waves and the squeals

of the gulls—sounds that used to remind me of family holidays at Treachery Bay—now created a very different atmosphere. The waves kept rolling in, relentless and oncoming, like the criminals who were after me, and the gulls shrieked and swooped, like birds of prey.

8:03 am

A sudden scraping noise from the driveway jolted my body into defensive action. I tore the blankets off me, hobbled on aching legs to the front drapes and cautiously peered around.

It was Boges's uncle! He was unloading cleaning gear from the back of his station wagon!

Instinctively I grabbed my mobile and switched it on, forgetting it had died on me. I was shocked when it actually flashed on for a second, before blacking out again. I snatched up all of my stuff and on my way to hide in the linen closet I grabbed the portable house phone that was hanging in the kitchen.

'What are you doing ringing me on this phone?' Boges's alarmed voice shouted down the line. 'What did I tell you about—'

'Boges, quit talking and listen for a sec,' I whispered. 'Your uncle Sammy's here! My phone got drenched; I didn't know what else to do. He's on his way in right now and—'

'Where are you?'

'Hiding in the closet! Do something!' I urged. 'Please!'

Boges swore and hung up the phone. I cowered in the back of the closet, running a check on whether I'd left anything incriminating lying in the living room. I had a sick feeling of déjà vu—I'd been in this situation way too many times to count.

I could hear the clanging sound of equipment being unloaded. As I tossed up whether I should bolt out the back of the property, I heard a mobile phone ring outside.

The voice that answered the call was only faint, but it was loud enough for me to know it was Sammy, talking in Ukrainian. His tone was frustrated, agitated.

There were some muffled sounds for a couple of minutes, which ended with the slamming of the car boot. Then the engine started, and the car drove away.

I crept out of the closet and back to my surveillance position behind the drapes. I watched as Sammy's white station wagon drove onto the street. I was alone again.

The house phone rang and I snatched it up.

'Boges?'

'Cal, what if that wasn't me ringing?!'

'You wanted me to answer it, didn't you? Anyway, I don't know what you said to him, but he's gone. He just left. He sounded annoyed.'

'I know. I told him I had a message from the owners that I'd completely forgotten to give him. I said they didn't want the cleaning done yet because they had a relative arriving to stay a few nights while in town for a conference. I said they wanted him to clean the place after their guest had left.'

'How did you come up with that?' I said, impressed with my friend's endless quick thinking.

'I don't even know!' Boges laughed. 'I rang him as soon as I got off the phone from you and made it up as I went along! He wasn't happy. With me *or* the owners of the house! Anyway, you're in the clear there for at least another six nights. Promise I'll give you the heads-up next time my uncle's on his way.'

I quickly gave Boges the run-down on everything that had happened since stealing the Jewel from Sligo.

'Can't wait to see it,' said Boges. 'Now that we have both parts of the double-key code maybe we can make sense of all the drawings.' I hoped he was right. 'We've gotta meet up, but people know I'm a link to you and I've gotta be way careful. Wherever I go these days, I feel like someone's watching me. I've seen Bruno a couple of times, and Zombie—Zombrovski—driving past, pretending to ignore me. They still haven't worked out my backyard escape route, although I had to do some more fast-talking the other day—my neighbour found me running across her yard. She started shouting at me, but I'd thrown a tennis ball into her bushes a little while ago, in case she ever found me, and I pretended I'd jumped the fence to get it back.' Boges stopped to laugh. 'I'm becoming a master of lying to get myself outta trouble!'

'Yeah, sorry about that,' I said, feeling a bit guilty about the life I'd forced my friend into. 'So when can we meet?' I was trying to think of a safe place, somewhere other than here at the mansion. 'Somewhere like the cinemas? Even if you're followed,' I continued, 'whoever is on your tail could think you're really just going to the movies, not meeting me. But if they do spot us together, it'll be easier to shake them off there.'

'OK, that could work.'

'How about tomorrow at the shops, downstairs at the cinema complex?'

'Can't get out until next week. How about Wednesday? After school? I'm too busy this weekend with family stuff, and then assignments. Plus I have that internship application to finish. It's making me tear my hair out.'

'Could be an improvement,' I joked. 'Wednesday it is.'

'Cool,' he said, ignoring my comment about his hair. 'Let's make it four o'clock. In the meantime, I'll to have to figure out a way to delete the record of these calls we've made. And if I need to call you before Wednesday, I'll call the house phone for two short rings, and then one long. Answer it on the third, OK?'

'Deal. Make sure your uncle doesn't come back any time soon, will ya?'

7:07 pm

I pulled the heavy drapes closed and watched the news on the TV near the kitchen. After a few international stories, a familiar shopfront appeared on the screen—Mike's Seafood. A senior officer stood outside, surrounded by a crowd of journalists with microphones. Questions were being thrown at him from all angles, but he ignored them. All he said was, 'We are confident we will catch Ormond very soon.'

Not if I had any say in the matter.

Then, as I expected, the grainy photo of me, deep in the freezer room, came up on the screen. *Three-O*, the dirty rat, had handed in the picture he took of me before locking me up. The next shot that came up was of the blasted freezer room door, and a cop holding up what was left of one of the track detonators. The camera panned back to the crowd outside the fish shop and I saw the rat standing next to Mike amongst the hungry journalists, all scavenging for a piece of the story.

Luckily the photo Three-O had taken was pretty bad and my face wasn't very clear. I was relieved he'd failed to get the cops there in time to cuff me, and I was just as relieved he didn't get the reward money out of it. Still, he had a hundred thousand reasons for trying to track me down to finish what he'd started.

8:40 pm

I sat for ages, staring at the crashing waves. I was trying to put everything out of my mind, so I started wandering around the house, looking for a distraction.

No-one would believe I was hiding out in a seven-bedroom, five-bathroom mansion, filled with fancy furniture and rugs, elaborate chandeliers and glass sculptures, huge paintings that were probably worth hundreds of thousands of dollars . . . There was even a theatre room with three raised rows of rich red, cinema-style recliner chairs in front of a huge movie screen. I was almost completely out of money, my clothes were getting shabbier with every day, I was a hunted fugitive and yet, thanks to Boges, I was sitting in a house fit for a prince.

I had to take advantage of it.

9:29 pm

I paid really careful attention to everything I did, so that I could leave the room exactly as it was before I entered it. Then I plonked myself down on a recliner, front row, centre.

I'd picked out a movie from the collection that made me think of Winter—*Bonnie and Clyde*. Winter and I shared such a strange connection—we were both different, we were both like outlaws, on our own. Had she really known about the Jewel all along, and lied to me about it? The picture of her I'd seen in Sligo's safe—wearing the Jewel—didn't make any sense. She had seemed so committed to getting me into Sligo's place, and out of there in one piece with the Jewel in *my* possession.

Anyway, I thought to myself, I had to put that mystery out of my mind for now—I had a movie to watch.

3 JULY

182 days to go . . .

4:35 am

I woke up in a sweat and quickly scrambled off the recliner chair I was sprawled on. I'd let myself fall asleep after watching the movie last night, but my old nightmare had returned and sent my mind into a spin.

Weird shadows filled the spacious room. I jumped up and went to the living room, back to my place on the rug, still trying to shake the white toy dog and the wailing baby from my head. When the sound wouldn't go away, I realised a real baby was crying, far away in a neighbouring property. Huddled against the wall, I tried telling myself everything was all right.

I couldn't fool myself. I was still haunted by the dark and desolate nightmare—its thick atmosphere wouldn't let me go. The world of the nightmare was too similar to the world I was sitting in right now—with a dark, deserted house, and the sound of a baby crying. Someone lost and abandoned. Someone exactly like me.

My mind flashed back to the 'Twin Baby Abduction Nightmare' article I'd seen at Great-uncle Bartholomew's house.

What had he been hiding, and why?

Did those babies have something to do with me . . . and my recurring nightmare? When Bartholomew was dying, had he meant to say that one of them was me? Or had that been a slip of the tongue? A sick feeling in my gut grew the more I thought about it. It was starting to feel way too personal.

Twin baby. The face of my double hovered in my consciousness. He had my face.

Dad and Rafe were twins.

Was I?

The thought of having a long-lost twin seemed impossible. If only I could call my mum to ask her for the truth.

I fell back on my sleeping-bag. Right now, I couldn't deal with this.

5 JULY

180 days to go . . .

9:02 am

The house phone was ringing. I waited, hoping it would match Boges's code. After two short rings, followed by one long, I snatched it up.

'Eric Blair's back!' he said. 'I've been scoping out your dad's old office on my way to school, and this morning I saw some new guy heading up the stairs outside the building. Immediately he caught my attention—he looked a bit frail—like someone who hasn't seen the sun in a while.'

'Yeah?' I urged, excitement building.

'And then this woman,' Boges continued, 'ran up the stairs after him, calling out—wait for it—*Eric*!'

'No way!'

'Yes, way! It *has* to be him. You must try calling him again.'

'I will, I'll try on a public phone today.'

'Cool. I have to go, but I'll see you on Wednesday.'

1:09 pm

It took me quite a while to find a public phone in Crystal Beach, and I pounced on the first one I saw, dialling Eric with flying fingers.

'Eric Blair, please,' I said when the receptionist picked up. I noted it was a new voice, and was relieved I didn't have to deal with the suspicious woman from my last call.

'One moment,' came the reply.

I waited, wondering what in the world I was going to say to him. I'd been anticipating this moment for so long, but hadn't figured out a strategy. I had no idea how he was going to react to hearing from me.

'Thank you for holding,' the voice returned, like a recording. 'Transferring you through.'

I could hardly believe it. Finally, I was getting the chance to talk to the guy that had been with Dad in Ireland, when he got sick.

'Eric Blair speaking.' His voice was tentative and gentle. 'Hello?'

'Mr Blair,' I said, 'I've been trying to get in touch with you for quite some time . . .' I faltered, completely freaking out about what to say.

'Yes, and how can I help you?'

'Please don't hang up on me when I tell you who I am—I really need your help, and have been counting on you for information.'

'Information on what?' he asked in a voice that was a little more familiar to me. He'd always sounded very confident and straightforward when I'd taken calls for Dad back home, way before the illness took hold.

'I'm Tom Ormond's son.'

There was a long silence at the other end before he spoke again.

'Cal?'

'Yes.'

'Cal. I'm really sorry about what happened to your father. I was unwell myself, and have been a bit . . . . umm . . . out of touch, but I know that you're in trouble. It's only my first day back in the office, so I can't really talk to you right now, but you should give me your number and we can chat another time.'

'Please,' I said. 'I have so many questions about what happened in Ireland. And don't believe what you've heard about me. None of it's true.'

He took down my mobile number and we hung up.

It wasn't until I was halfway back to the mansion that I realised I'd given him a number he couldn't even call me on.

7 JULY

178 days to go . . .

Star Cinemas

3:48 pm

Shortly before four o'clock, I waited for Boges near the busy ticket line. I kept my head down and avoided eye contact, following the rule of the street. Nobody took any notice of me standing there like anyone else waiting for a friend to show up for a movie.

Somehow I'd managed to shove all thoughts of that haunting 'Twin Baby Abduction Nightmare' headline into the deepest corner of my mind, but it hadn't been so easy to squeeze Winter in there with it. I couldn't get her floaty hair and tiny bird tattoo out of my mind, and I couldn't stop picturing the photo I'd seen of her in the silver dress wearing the Ormond Jewel around her neck. If she knew about it all along, why didn't she just say so? And then why did she help us steal it? There had to be another expla-

141

nation. Without her help, we never could have penetrated Sligo's security to get into the safe.

4:11 pm

Boges hadn't shown up yet, and I wished he'd hurry. This wait in public was doing my head in. I was thinking about the mysterious warning I'd received: *If the heir dies before his sixteenth birthday . . .*

I didn't know what 'the heir' in the message was about, but my sixteenth birthday, 31 July, was coming up fast. I couldn't help but believe it referred to me, and that right now I was a bigger target than ever.

July also meant the anniversary of Dad's death. He died only a matter of days before my birthday, which meant that my fifteenth had been absolutely miserable.

The memory of it returned as if it had happened yesterday. Mum was like a ghost, filled with grief, drifting around the house like a lost soul. She and Gabbi tried so hard to make my birthday count—they even baked me a cake and gave me an awesome skateboard—but it was way too soon. The house was still fresh with the scent of flowers from Dad's funeral.

When the three of us sat at the table, lit up by the glow of the candles on my birthday cake, the empty chair was all we could focus on.

Gabbi stared at it with longing. 'It's not fair,' she'd cried. 'How can anyone have a birthday without Dad? Why did he have to leave us like this? It's just not fair!'

Mum put her arms around both of us, pulling us tight. Through tears she said that he'd always be there, in our hearts. She said that we'd all have to be strong and go on without him; we'd have to be there for each other, because he would be so sad if he saw us falling apart.

4:15 pm

Something vibrated in my bag. Confused, I dug my mobile out, and was shocked to see a glimmer of life on the stained screen—someone had just sent me a message.

I fumbled, trying to see if there was a number with it, but the phone blacked out again. I looked around, worried—was I being watched right now? Was a skull on a lifeless phone a warning?

I pulled my hoodie around my face and quickly walked away from the cinema. At the first side street I started running, not stopping until I was five or six blocks away in the area around Central Station, where I ducked into a phone booth and called Boges.

'Someone's just messaged me—sent me a pic of a skull, saying "Gotcha"! I bolted from the cinemas, and right now I'm in a phone booth at the station. I didn't even think my mobile was working!'

'You've gotta lose that mobile! I'll get you another one,' said Boges. 'How did anyone get your number?'

'Maybe Sligo's on to Winter. Maybe he knows that she's been helping me, and he got into her phone.'

'Maybe she *gave* it to him.'

'No way. She's on our side, not his,' I said. I still hadn't told Boges about the photo of Winter I'd found in the safe, but I was feeling more protective of her than ever—I feared what Sligo would do to her if he found out she'd been assisting his enemy.

Boges had been held up at home and it was too late now for me to double back to the cinema and meet him. We agreed to meet up tomorrow, at a new location. He told me again to get rid of the phone in case someone, somehow, was tracking it.

I did better than lose it. It took me about three minutes to dodge security, jump the station ticket barriers and run down to one of the platforms. No-one even noticed as I slipped my phone through one of the windows of the train, and disappeared again.

If Sligo or Oriana de la Force were able to get a GPS reading on my half-dead mobile, they'd think I was heading west, fast.

I'd learned something from Bartholomew and Maggers.

8 JULY

177 days to go . . .

Storage Giant

3:56 pm

Approaching the address Boges had given me, I found myself in an industrial area with the occasional block of apartments between warehouses and bulk storage buildings.

I didn't recognise Boges immediately. As I came closer, he pushed himself away from the wall where he'd been leaning, dangling a key. He was wearing mirrored sunglasses and white overalls. Beside him were his bag and some paint tins.

'Uncle Sammy's got a storage unit here,' he said, grinning. 'It's pretty big. He asked me to drop off these paint tins. Saves me drawing any attention to the mansion by visiting you there. Quick, chuck this on,' he said, throwing me a pair of white overalls like his. 'Better make it look like we both mean business.'

I glanced around, making sure no-one was looking, then stepped into the overalls.

Boges unlocked the security grille at the front of the block, and we wandered down to his uncle's unit. He unlocked the garage door, rolled it up and we stepped inside. Then he flicked a light switch on and pulled the roller door back down.

The room was fairly empty, aside from a couple of industrial vacuum cleaners, crates and other boxes.

'You'll need this. It's clean,' said Boges, handing me another phone from his pocket, along with a piece of paper with the number written on it. 'Only you and I know the number. Keep it that way.' He gave me a look from under his sunglasses and pulled a couple of crates towards us to sit on. 'The cops can sometimes pinpoint where a mobile is being used, but they need your number first. I'm afraid there's only one person who could have double-crossed you . . .'

'Winter risked everything to help us get the Jewel,' I said, defensively.

'Whether or not she was involved,' he said impatiently, 'the fact is that Sligo's getting awfully close to you. Dude, I hate to say it, but I think he wants to rub you out before your sixteenth birthday.'

I nodded, knowing what he was saying was probably true, before moving the conversation away from that grim idea. 'I phoned Eric Blair,' I said. 'He said he'd call me back—it was only his first day back in the office.'

'What do you mean, he's going to *call you*?'

'He was flat out, so I gave him my—oh crap,' I said, remembering that Winter clearly wasn't the only person I'd given my number to. 'But my phone wasn't even working—I didn't think he'd be able to call me.'

Boges shook his head. He looked angry. He stood up and started pacing around the room. 'What are you doing, giving him your number? As far as he knows you've tried to murder your own family! Yeah, he was mates with your dad, but you don't have a clue yet whether you can trust him! He could have gone straight to the cops! What if he sent the skull message?'

Boges stopped pacing. He put his hands on his hips and took a deep breath. 'Dude,' he said, calmly, 'you have to be more careful. Seriously. You can't trust anyone. OK?'

He was right. It was a stupid thing to do. 'You're right,' I finally agreed. 'Anyway, he doesn't have the right number any more. Thanks for this,' I said, pocketing the mobile. 'I want to get out of here—the city. I've gotta find Millicent.

Bartholomew thought she might have helpful information. It's weird, she's my great-aunt but I barely know anything about her.'

'Weird, yes,' Boges agreed. 'So you're going to visit her?' he asked, taking off the sunglasses and cocking his eyebrow. 'And *how* exactly?'

I was stumped.

'How about this then?' Boges pulled a sheet of folded paper out of his little black book, triumphantly slapping it down in my hand.

It was a directory webpage print-out, with a couple of lines highlighted in yellow.

'I searched for "Millicent Ormond" in an online country phone directory,' said Boges. 'And there she was! Finally something simple and straightforward. Kind of.'

Beside my great-aunt's name, fully printed out as 'Millicent Butler Ormond', was the address 'Manresa', Redcliffe.

'She must live on a property like "Kilkenny",' I said, thinking of Great-uncle Bartholomew's homestead that was now nothing more than charred ruins. 'All I have to do is find Redcliffe and then ask around for "Manresa".'

Boges pulled out his laptop and turned it to face me. 'Here's Redcliffe,' he said, pointing to a state map. 'It's way up there—in the north. A long way past Mount Helicon. About one hundred

kilometres inland from Paradise Beach. It's going
to be a long trip for you.'

'Boges, this is unreal. Thanks heaps.'

'No problem.'

Jumping trains, hitching rides, walking endless kilometres. One day, I promised myself, all
this running would be over. But until then, and
until I'd searched out the huge secret that Dad
had partly unearthed, I had to stay on the road,
stay alive, keep ahead of my enemies. *Three
hundred and sixty-five days*, the crazy guy
from New Year's Eve had warned. The mysterious Ormond Singularity was supposed to end
on December 31st too. I was more than halfway
through the year now, and I couldn't wait for the
day when I could clear my name and be safe at
home with my family. Mum, Gabbi and me.

'How are they?' I asked, straightening up. 'Mum
and Gabbi? I've been wanting to call, but . . .'

'Gabbi appears to be showing signs of life,
but she's still in the coma. Your mum and Rafe
latch onto every flicker of her eyelids, every
movement in her body, believing that one day
she'll come around. Your mum is looking after
her now at Rafe's place—apparently he's hired a
full-time specialist nurse for her. He even tore
the wall down between two of his upstairs rooms
to make one big room for Gab, one that fits her

bed, the hospital machinery and monitors. The doctors still say there is every chance of a full recovery. It's just an extremely slow process.'

'She's at Rafe's place?' I said, surprised.

'Yep. They think being in a home environment might help her wake up.'

'Has she spoken or anything yet?'

Boges scrunched up his face and shook his head.

'And Mum?' I asked. 'Is she any better?'

Boges hesitated. 'I would say she's doing fine. Your mum and Rafe—well—they seem to be getting along fine.'

My stomach muscles tightened at the way he said 'fine'.

'Fine?' I asked.

My friend squirmed uncomfortably, and then started scratching his head.

'How fine?' I repeated, bothered by the look on his face.

He turned away, clearly uncomfortable with my question. And that was answer enough. I didn't want to think about Mum and Rafe getting along. I was happy he was around to help her, to do all those awesome things to make Mum and Gab comfortable, like altering the house, but I just wanted everything to go back to how it was before. The fact that Rafe looked so much like Dad—he was his identical twin—made everything worse. It was like a parallel universe, where Dad had died and been replaced by a slightly different version of himself.

When Boges spoke again, his expression had changed.

'Let's get down to business. Come on, dude. Show it to me. At last I get to see this infamous Jewel.'

I pulled my backpack off and carefully pulled out the Ormond Jewel.

I held it out to him; it was as big as the palm of my hand, the oval emerald glowing.

Slowly, Boges picked it up and studied it as he turned it over in his hands. The rubies flashed like fire as he lifted the catch and opened it. Inside was the painted portrait of a woman with red-gold hair, a jewelled crown and necklace.

'Elizabeth the First of England,' said Boges.

He closed the heavy gold locket and put it down, but couldn't take his eyes off it. I couldn't either. It was mesmerising, filled with power. There was something about it that drew me to it, like a magnetic aura. It was like some sort of medieval transmitting device, pulsing out a huge, hidden secret, waiting hundreds of years to be joined with the old poem, and then decoded by just the right person.

'I'll tell you what I know,' I said. 'Great-uncle Bartholomew knew about it, but believed it had vanished long ago—broken up and sold. He had an old book that described it exactly, although it was written in old-fashioned language. He also said that the Ormond Riddle and the Ormond Jewel *are* the two halves of the double-key code.'

'Yes, so all we have to do is solve the Riddle, and crack the code, by putting it all together, somehow, with this awesome Jewel. Then we'll understand the Ormond Singularity. Mmmm,' said Boges. 'Sounds like you need yourself a genius,' he grinned.

'That's right. Any ideas on where we can find us a genius?'

Boges laughed and started sorting through his bag. 'All families have secrets,' he said, 'but it must be a big one if it's got all these barriers around it, protecting it.'

'And everyone trying to get their hands on it.'

Boges placed copies of the photos from Dad's memory stick on the concrete floor in front of me. 'I printed these out for you. Let's put the two halves of this double-key code together and see what we have.'

I pulled the drawings out, laying them in a row next to the Ormond Jewel. Then I laid the Riddle beside the shining Jewel.

'So what do we have so far?' I said, half asking myself. 'The Angel images led us to the Piers

Ormond memorial. We have the drawing that told us we were looking for something that could be worn—and that turned out to be a message telling us to find the Jewel. There's a connection between the drawing of the boy and the rose, and the rose on the back of the Jewel. There's the Sphinx—which could have been pointing to the Riddle, but I'm still not exactly sure about the Roman bust.' I tapped the drawing of the butler with the blackjack. 'Here I think Dad was trying to tell us about Black Tom Butler. The Queen gave this Jewel to one Black Tom, the tenth Earl of Ormond.'

'Man,' said Boges, looking up from the Jewel to me. 'Old Black Tom, eh? I feel like I'm handling a piece of history.'

'You are.' I felt a shiver of dangerous excitement. 'Everything here in front of us is trying to tell us what the secret is. Boges, it's all here.' I thought of the missing final lines of the riddle. 'Almost all here,' I corrected.

I stood up and walked around the room. I was starting to get edgy. I remembered my dad's eyes and the desperation in them as they followed me around his hospice room, after he returned from Ireland, sick. He had so much to tell me, but I just wasn't getting it.

Dad, help me.

I rearranged some of the drawings.

'Look,' said Boges, 'there's a "5" in your dad's drawing, and a "5" on the gate in his Ireland photos.' He leaned closer to the images and shifted a few more pages around. 'And your dad drew some sort of door, which could have been an attempt to send us to this wardrobe!' he said, pointing to the photo of the ornate piece of furniture that was also taken in Ireland. 'Hey, what happened to your hands?' asked Boges, suddenly noticing the fading cuts and scratches that were all over me from being netted and dumped on the deck of the *Star of Mykonos*.

I began by backtracking a bit and telling him in more detail about the carjacking I stupidly got involved in, courtesy of Griff Kirby, and everything that went on after the jewel heist with Repro. Then I explained what happened with the Southport Police—my crazy cop car and jet ski escape—getting caught by a fishing boat, and then ending up locked in the freezer at Mike's Seafood by Three-O.

'You're mixing with some seriously dangerous characters,' said Boges.

'They seem to mix with *me*. My job is to keep out of trouble—and to stay alive.'

'What happened with that ex-detective guy who contacted you on your blog?'

'Nelson Sharkey? Nothing, yet,' I replied, amazed at Boges's ability to remember so much when everything in my mind was completely chaotic.

I picked up the picture of Dad standing in front of a stony ruin. 'But once I talk to Eric—I'll be on guard, don't worry—I think he'll be able to fill in a lot of the gaps about what happened in Ireland when he was there with Dad. Plus I'm sure I'll find something in Redcliffe.'

'I think it's a good idea to get out of the city again. And now you have a clean mobile, so they can't get at you electronically either. You can access the internet on it too, so you don't need to risk going into any more internet cafés, OK?'

'Cool!' I said, pulling the phone out and looking at it more closely. 'How are you paying for all this?'

'It's taken care of. Don't worry about it. Here,' said Boges, passing me a hundred dollars. 'I should give you this before I change my mind!'

I looked at him in disbelief.

'I'm making heaps of money at the moment on eBay,' he explained, 'plus I have cash coming in from tutoring and the cleaning work with Uncle Sammy. I got that new mobile for you at a great price too—the seller thought it was too damaged to repair, but not too damaged for me! So now you have money, a clean phone, and a mission. And we're way ahead of the crims—we're the only people in the world who know about the meanings in these images,' he said, glancing at the display we'd made, 'and, of course, the double-key code.'

I was silent, knowing that wasn't true. Boges stared hard at me.

'We are the only people in the world, aren't we?'

'Winter knows about Black Tom and how the Riddle and the Jewel go together to make the double-key code.'

'*What?*'

'Calm down, it's OK,' I said. 'Winter Frey is cool. You don't know her like I do.'

'Clearly!' Boges jumped up off the floor and kicked a piece of scrap timber that had been used to stir paint. It hit the wall and bounced back, raising dust. 'I knew we should never have trusted that cheating, lying, double-crossing chick! You forget the name of the solicitor we need, but you don't forget to tell that sneaky chick everything we know! She gets around looking all fancy, wearing shiny stuff in her hair like she thinks she's some little angel, and pretends to help us while all the time she's playing us for fools! She's trying to work up a fake friendship with you, and then behind your back she runs to Sligo with every scrap of information. Have you got some kind of death wish?'

'Hold up, *she's* the one who told *us* about the double-key code! You're way out of line, Boges,' I said, angry at my friend's outburst. 'You don't know Winter like I do.'

He turned his attention back to his laptop.

'Incredible,' he said after a minute or two, his eyes wide in surprise at something he'd just seen on the screen. 'Don't even think of calling her!' he shouted as I peered over his shoulder.

Web | Images | Video | News | Maps | More ⌄

Web Search

Hello, Callum

Contact Cal
Messages for Cal

Inbox | Sent | Drafts

From: Love_Little_Bird

Love_Little_Bird

Been trying to call you—what's happened, you OK? It's really weird I haven't heard from you. Call me.

W.F.

If only Boges knew about the photo in the safe. That was the only reason I hadn't called Winter. I turned the laptop back to him without commenting, even though inside I felt like I wanted to call *Little Bird* more than ever.

After another minute, he directed the screen to me once more.

EWS! BREAKING NEWS! >> Ormond keeps Police guessing >> Fugitive still on the

Murderer-Turned-Blogger Taunts Police

Thurs 8 Jul, 14:27

Wanted teen Cal Ormond, notorious for a trail of destruction across the state including murder and attempted murder, has been posting messages on an online blog, claiming innocence, while taunting the authorities.

Callum Ormond: Not as innocent as he looks

'Psychopaths often like to toy with the police,' said Chief Superintendent Arnie Broadhurst today, 'but we're closing in on him. It's only a matter of time before we'll have him behind bars.'

The dangerous juvenile recently evaded police custody, when posing as an escaped mental patient, Benjamin Galloway. Chief Superintendent Broadhurst insists they have a strong lead and are expecting an arrest shortly. Police presence on roads leading out of the city has been increased.

Related articles
Back to Top | Next

I read the last sentence again and swore. It was going to be hard getting to Millicent.

'I'd better go,' I said, gathering everything up. I hesitated for a moment before handing it all over to Boges. 'I don't want to carry this with me on the road to Redcliffe—could you look after it for me?'

Boges nodded, silently shut down his laptop and then loaded up his backpack. I trusted him more than anyone else, but handing it all over felt like I was losing a part of myself.

I ended up taking back the drawings. They were all I had left that connected me to my dad.

We walked to the door and both pulled it up. I was half-expecting sunlight to stream through, but it was well and truly dark now.

Boges patted his backpack protectively, acknowledging the importance of what was concealed inside. He put out his hand to shake mine.

'Good luck, buddy.'

9 JULY
176 days to go . . .

S Enid Parade, Crystal Beach

11:56 am

As soon as I heard her voice on the other end of the line, my gut churned with strange, mixed-up feelings of excitement and suspicion. I needed to know what she had to say about the photo of her wearing the Jewel.

'It's Cal,' I said.

'About time!' said Winter. 'I've been dying to talk to you—I heard something important about the Jewel.'

'Go on.'

'It has something written inside,' she said. 'I heard Sligo talking about it on the phone to someone—about an inscription. He said it was "a crucial guide".'

'Guide to what?'

'He didn't say.' She paused at the end of the line. 'What's wrong?'

'I saw a photo of you in Sligo's safe.'

'What in the world are you talking about, Callum Ormond?'

'You were wearing a silver dress . . . and around your neck you were *wearing* the Ormond Jewel.'

'*What?*'

Her surprise sounded genuine.

'You heard me. I want to know why you pretended you had never seen the Ormond Jewel. I want to know why you lied to me.'

'Cal, I didn't lie to you! I've never even seen the Jewel! Do you think I wouldn't tell you if I had? Why would I help you get inside Sligo's—put myself in serious danger—' She inhaled loudly before speaking again. 'This is ridiculous!'

'But you were wearing—'

'I don't even know what you're talking about! It never happened. Got it? *Never* happened.'

'I saw it with my own eyes.'

There was a pause. 'Cal, I think I know what's happened.' Winter spoke slowly, as if thinking out loud. 'Sligo had my photo taken last year in my favourite silver dress. It was a portrait—by a professional photographer—but I definitely wasn't wearing *anything* around my neck. Not even Mum and Dad's locket.'

'So how do you explain the photo I saw?'

'Wake up, Cal! People can do anything with digital photo editing! This is so typical of Sligo and his pathetic dream of becoming respectable! You know he wants to host the New Year's Eve Council Ball. He wants to sit up there with the city councillors, parading me on one side and the Mayor on the other. He's always going on about visualising your dreams to make them happen—he probably made the picture up as part of that belief! Don't you see?'

I thought back to the picture and recalled that it had looked grainy. Was she telling the truth? I was sick of the trust in our friendship see-sawing, and I really wanted to believe her.

I had a strong sense that she was telling the truth.

'Just when I thought we were getting close, something else throws you into a spin . . . I *so* want to see the Ormond Jewel,' she continued. 'And I want to see you. I've been working on the Riddle and I've had some thoughts on solving it. We need to meet up. To talk about everything.'

'What ideas have you had?'

'Look, I don't want to discuss them on the phone. But I really think I'm on to something, Cal. There's a portrait of the Queen inside the Jewel, right?'

'Yes.'

'I also have some ideas about that.'

I really wanted to see her, but I couldn't quite shake all my suspicions. Boges's doubts had rubbed off on me.

'I'm going to be—' I hesitated, unsure as to how much I should reveal about my trip to Redcliffe, '*occupied* for a while,' I said. 'Let's meet up when I'm free, down the track. We can put our heads together and see what we can come up with.'

'I'd like that,' she said. I could almost feel her smile coming down the line. 'You have my number. Don't forget to use it.'

13 JULY

172 days to go . . .

4:00 pm

It was time for me to leave the mansion and make my way to Redcliffe. I kissed the rug, the five bathrooms and the home theatre goodbye, and headed towards Central Station with my backpack, full of supplies, and sleeping-bag in tow. I wasn't feeling very confident about getting through security, but had to give it a go.

I was hoping I could somehow sneak into Central Station and jump on a train that would take me at least part of the way to Redcliffe. But as soon as I reached the huge entrance hall of the station, I saw a stack of new security cameras, and cops on patrol. Hurriedly, I backed away.

A black van cruised up alongside me. I looked hard through the windscreen and nearly died when I saw who was driving it—Sligo's body-guard, Zombrovski! He swerved the car towards me, forcing me to dive aside to dodge it!

I got up and took a flying leap over the stone

wall that separated the road and the station ramp from the basketball courts. It was a drop of about two metres, but I had to get away from the road! I hit the ground hard, tumbling and rolling before getting back up and running through the gate in the wire that enclosed the courts.

The only other exit in the wire was diagonal from where I'd entered. I bolted towards it, hoping to escape down the street it opened onto. I dashed recklessly past a group of kids, sending their basketballs bouncing in all directions. I ignored their shouts as I focused on the gate, but I couldn't ignore the black van that had driven into view! I skidded to a halt—it looked like Zombie was talking on a phone. Calling for reinforcements? I was going to have to go back towards the gate I'd just come through!

As soon as I started running back to the first gate, I saw the van U-turn and speed back up the road, preparing to catch me at the other end again.

I skidded, changing direction once more, but this time I was faced with another, even more serious problem—Sligo's black Subaru was now covering the second exit! I was trapped!

The tall wire mesh that enclosed the basketball courts had become a cage! It was hopeless!

I stood there panting, not knowing what

move to make next, when a pigeon fluttered up past my line of sight. I followed its path with my eyes, which led me to a large hole in a corner of the wire, way up high. I had no alternative and couldn't waste any time, so I threw myself at the wire and climbed like a mad monkey until I'd reached the opening. I squeezed through and flung my body out the other side, half climbing, half falling to the ground.

I landed a few metres from a bus stop where a bunch of kids, who looked like a team of basketballers, were noisily boarding a bus. To my right, I saw the van turn the corner, coming my way. It was getting dark, so I hoped they hadn't spotted me behind the group.

'Hurry up, boys,' said a nearby voice. 'Come along. Just get on board. We should have left fifteen minutes ago. Are you part of this excursion group?'

I swung round to see that the teacher, a young guy with a scarf and a clipboard in his hand, was talking to me!

'Yes sir,' I said, making a split-second decision to try the bus as cover. I didn't think I had a hope on foot with the Subaru and the van in pursuit.

I joined the kids as they boarded, my eyes scanning to see where my hunters were.

'Hurry up!' the man with the clipboard repeated.

I didn't need to be told again. I squeezed in, noticing that the kids must have been from different schools—they all had different school crests on their backpacks. There were a couple of kids keeping to themselves, too, so I guessed not everyone knew each other. Perfect.

Squashed and sweaty in one of the seats, I saw the black van cruise right past the bus.

I let out a huge sigh of relief. For the moment I was safe.

From the talk around me, I gathered I was with a group of basketballers who were heading north for a sports camp. The guy beside me had earphones in, listening to music so loud that even I could hear it. I was glad he wasn't interested in talking; it gave me some time to let my heart rate settle and concentrate on blocking out the memory that had resurfaced, of seeing my double at the courts, months ago.

7:10 pm

After a couple of hours, everyone had quietened down a bit. I started getting edgy again, worried someone would start taking more of an interest in me. I couldn't afford having anyone look too closely at me.

Just as we were about to pull into a roadside restaurant for dinner, I noticed a group of three guys whispering. They were trying hard not to look at me, but I knew I was the topic under discussion.

I didn't want to make too obvious an exit, so I waited for the bus to stop, then slipped out behind some of the taller guys who were pushing and shoving their way off. As soon as I could, I ducked around the back of the bus and ran into the night.

8:05 pm

After walking through the dark for a while, I saw red and blue lights flashing down from the highway. I crept behind some thick, prickly bushes and peered out.

A police roadblock had slowed a line of cars down to a crawl. Every car was being stopped and searched.

I put my hand into my pocket and touched the small angel pin Repro had given me. It had given me plenty of good luck so far; I hoped it would continue on my way to reach Millicent.

The night was cold and dark, with a waning moon sinking in the sky. I tried not to think of this time last year, when Dad was dying, but I kept being haunted by those memories. I wished I'd been able to say to him: 'I get it, Dad. I understand what you're trying to tell me. I will continue the search to uncover the truth about the Ormond Singularity, and I promise to protect what's left of our family.' Maybe that would have given him some comfort as he died.

I looked up at the immense sky, filled with brilliant stars in the blackness of deep space. I shifted my backpack on my shoulders, preparing to walk long into the night. I didn't know exactly where I was—but I still had a long way to go before I made it to Redcliffe.

17 JULY

168 days to go . . .

10:00 pm

Right now I was lying under the stars, praying it wouldn't rain, and thinking about how my life had turned out so far. I'd been on the road for over three days, walking as far as my legs would carry me by day, and then sleeping in the bush, or wherever I could find a soft, quiet place, when it got dark.

Going to school and coming home to my family seemed such a long, long time ago.

Every now and then, more times than I liked, Winter came into my mind. I realised I would probably never figure her out, and while that drove me nuts, it was also kind of what I liked about her.

18 JULY

167 days to go . . .

Redcliffe

5:14 pm

At last, I'd arrived in Redcliffe. It was another quiet, rural town in the foothills of the mountains.

I stopped and sat down on a bench next to a lonely town monument. I switched on the new mobile Boges had given me, and sent him a text message.

📱 made it

Next, I entered my blog address, hoping I had enough coverage. It was taking some time to load.

I swung round, spooked by a distant siren, and started walking again.

Down the road was a sleepy country graveyard, with mossy headstones leaning at crooked angles and a small chapel among some trees.

Eventually, my blog page loaded up, and I clicked on another private message from Winter.

Web Search

Hello, Callum

Contact Cal
Messages for Cal

Inbox Sent Drafts

From: Love_Little_Bird

Love_Little_Bird

You are in great danger. What's written on the OJ relates to the OS. VS wants it back more than ever. He has people searching for you. They have some leads on your location, I don't know where from. *Please call me. Please trust me. Everything depends on this.*

Love, Little Bird

I dialled Boges as I stepped into the grave-yard, stopping at a secluded spot behind the chapel, where a stone wall hid me from view. There was no answer.

If what Winter Frey said was true, and Sligo had some leads on where I was, it could mean only a matter of time before tracing me to Great-aunt Millicent, and to Redcliffe.

Fear gripped me.

He might have found her already.

Anxious to move faster, I spotted a guy working at the end of the stone wall, ripping out blackberry bushes. He stopped what he was doing when he saw me, straightening up and pulling off his thick gloves.

'Excuse me,' I said, 'I'm looking for a property called "Manresa". Do you know where it is?'

The guy looked surprised, pushing hair off his sweaty forehead.

'Manresa? What business do you have there?'

'Visiting a relative,' I said. 'Why? Is there a problem?'

He raised an eyebrow but didn't answer my question; instead, he picked up a long stick and began drawing a rough map in the dirt at his feet.

'You keep going along this road, until you pass a couple of big homesteads. You can't miss them. Then you take a turn left here,' he said, branching out with another line, 'and keep going another couple of kilometres. Manresa's right at the end.'

'Thanks, buddy,' I said.

He was still looking at me strangely. 'You sure it was Manresa you were after?' he said, before his phone rang and he waved me on.

6:43 pm

I set off as the evening drew in, keeping the rough map in my mind. Storm clouds were gathering over the mountains and distant lightning split the air. Growls of thunder made me go faster. I was cold enough already. I didn't want to get drenched as well.

After following the gardener's instructions, I came to a small, faded signpost, pointing down a dirt track, which spelled out the name 'Manresa'. I wondered what sort of place it was, hidden away on the edges of a small country town like Redcliffe.

I wrapped my hoodie tightly around me against the wind, and cautiously jogged down the track. I kept going over and over Winter's message. I'd never noticed anything written on the Ormond Jewel, and neither had Boges, so I didn't know what she could have been talking about.

A couple of lights shone in the distance, urging me to rush on. I hoped my great-aunt was OK, and that Sligo's stooges hadn't beaten me to her. I also wondered if she'd heard the news about her brother's death. I sure didn't want to be the one to tell her.

The wind suddenly stopped and the storm that had been threatening broke overhead, sending rain pelting down, hard and cold. Within seconds I was soaked, and the dusty surface of the road had turned into treacherous mud.

I kept running until I reached the iron and stone pillar fencing that circled the large building. The structure was imposing in the evening light, half-hidden behind tall, leafless trees. Some sort of spire reached high into the sky, and a driveway curved up and around the entrance, making the place look like some kind of institution—an institution like Leechwood Lodge. Was my great-aunt insane?

Another sign, now dripping with water, swung on the front gates. I rubbed some dirt from it and squinted in the poor light, trying to read it. I could hardly believe my eyes!

'Manresa Convent,' I read. 'Enclosed order of the Sisters of Sancta Sophia.'

Great-aunt Millicent lived in a convent?

Would I even be allowed into an enclosed order? Didn't that mean that the nuns had virtually no contact with the outside world?

Then it struck me: this could be the one place in the country that hadn't heard about me—Cal Ormond, Psycho Kid.

A figure was heading down the driveway towards me. She was an elderly nun with a black umbrella. Her robes flapped in the wind, and raindrops shone on her black veil. Behind her, the convent loomed, dark and mysterious.

'What are you doing here? Who are you?' the

nun demanded, her sharp eyes in her wrinkled face checking me out.

I took a deep breath and a risk. 'My name is Cal Ormond,' I said.

She held the umbrella out and I stepped under it with her.

'You can talk to me while I close the gates for the night,' she said, straining to make her voice heard above the rain. 'But first, please tell me what you're doing here.'

'I'm trying to find my great-aunt, Millicent Ormond,' I said. 'This is the address I was given for her. I must talk with her. It's concerning a very urgent family matter.'

'Millicent, you say?' she asked, before making a humming, thinking kind of sound as she bolted the gates I'd come through. 'Do you mean Sister Mary Perpetua?'

'Mary Perpetua? No, I don't know who she is. My great-aunt's name is Millicent Butler Ormond,' I said. 'She's my dad's aunt.'

'Come in out of the rain, boy,' said the nun, looking me up and down again and leading us with a tilt of the umbrella. She looked pretty old, but her eyes were bright and her step was brisk as we walked quickly towards an open door on the side of the stone building. 'When we come into the convent,' she explained, 'we take another name. Your aunt took "Perpetua". It means "eternal".'

Eternal. I thought of Sligo's 'leads' and pictured Bruno or Zombrovski heading this way. I hoped it didn't mean eternal rest.

'I don't know what I'm going to do with you,' the nun said, as we hurried up the front steps, 'but it would be most un-Christian of me to leave you out here in this weather.'

I followed the nun to the heavy double doors, noticing a huge, gleaming brass bell hanging in the tower above the entrance steps. The steps were hemmed in by cactus plants, much taller than us, each one sprouting several long, stiff arms covered in wickedly sharp-looking thorns. They reminded me of giant sea urchins, with their massive, spiky arms spreading in all directions.

Through the doors was a cavernous entry hall. It was a gloomy, cathedral-like area, dimly lit with three wavering candles burning in front of the statue of a saint—a guy in armour who was standing in an alcove set in the wall. Next to the alcove were dangling ropes and the narrow bell tower stairs. I shivered, not only because of the cold. Something about being there reminded me of what it was like in the Ormond mausoleum, with the bones of my ancestors.

I stopped at the first of the three candles, my

attention caught by the very real-looking sword that was attached to the armoured saint's right hand, held in place only by some thin wire.

'Cool sword,' I said, admiring its blade, gleaming in the candlelight.

'Saint Ignatius, bless him,' muttered the nun. 'A warrior saint. And yes, that sword—it *is* real. It was a gift from a benefactor—a military man. A general,' she explained as she led me further inside, shaking water from the folds in her clothes as she walked. I followed her down a passageway and into a large kitchen area at the end.

'Thanks for letting me in,' I said, pulling off my drenched hoodie. We walked to a large table in the middle of the kitchen, where a large slow-combustion stove warmed us. The walls were covered in old-fashioned copper cooking utensils and the counters were stacked with piles of clean plates. The kitchen smelled of a thousand meals.

'You're lucky I saw you when I did. If I hadn't been shutting the gates, you'd still be out there in the rain, I'm afraid.' She put out her right hand to shake mine. 'I'm Sister Jerome. I fetch the shopping and answer the front door for the other sisters, among other things, of course. I drive the minibus, too. Where are you from, child?'

'Here and there. I sort of—camp out.'

'You've been sleeping rough? In this cold weather? Where's your mother? You look like you could do with a good bath, and I'd better find something for you to wear. You'll catch your death in those wet clothes!'

She draped my wet hoodie over the back of the chair closest to the stove.

'Thank you, Sister, but I have some extra clothes here,' I said, digging around in my backpack to find something else to put on. 'Could you please tell my great-aunt that I'm here and I would like to talk with her? It's extremely important.'

Sister Jerome had a worried look on her face.

'Has anybody else been here?' I asked. 'Wanting to speak with Millicent? Sorry, Sister Mary Perpetua?'

'Certainly not. How come?'

'I need to talk to her. To tell her something,' I continued, 'and ask her something about an important family matter.'

'A family matter? We nuns don't have families. We're about the last of the old, enclosed orders. We still live by the old-fashioned rules. We leave that entire muddle behind us. As the great Saint Teresa said, "Not being able to have contact with your families is often a great blessing".' She gave me a stern look. 'You know what families can be like.'

She had a point, but I could never imagine turning my back on my family for good.

'This is really important. Because there could be—a problem,' I added, not wanting to alarm her.

'What problem?'

How could I tell her that any number of bloodthirsty criminals could be on their way here right now, trying to chase me down, without a care for anyone standing in their way? She'd never believe me.

'Never mind,' I said. 'I'm just really looking forward to seeing her.'

8:29 pm

Sister Jerome showed me the outdoor bathroom and I washed up a bit in a big laundry near the kitchen. I paused to look at my reflection in a speckled mirror. My long, lank, dirty blond hair looked darker than ever.

Five minutes later I was sitting in the kitchen of the Manresa Convent in a dry grey sweater from my backpack, while Sister Jerome cut me a jam sandwich and made hot chocolate. I liked the way she locked the kitchen door behind me as I returned. I was in a holy, stone fortress, surrounded by a spiky cactus moat, a group of

nuns, and strong locks. This had to be the ulti-
mate safe house.

'Now you wait there and eat up,' she said,
pointing to the sandwich, 'while I go and find
out what's to be done with you.'

I tucked into it, greedily. From somewhere I
could hear the sound of chanting and I guessed
it was the nuns singing.

By the time I'd finished eating and was halfway through my drink, Sister Jerome was back.
She frowned solemnly.

'I'm afraid you are going to be disappointed.
I didn't want to mention it earlier, but I fear you
have come all this way for nothing.'

'For nothing? Please don't stop me from speaking to my great-aunt!' I pleaded. 'This is way too
important!'

'Nobody's going to stop you, Cal,' she said with
a gentle hand on my shoulder. 'There's something you should know.'

My heart sank. I waited for her to tell me
that Millicent was dead.

'Sister Mary Perpetua—your great-aunt—she
doesn't speak any more. In fact, she hasn't spoken for an exceptionally long time. I think it was
about twenty years ago that she stopped.'

'What?' I asked, putting the mug of hot
chocolate down. 'Why?' I was torn between being

relieved she was alive, and confused as to why she had stopped speaking.

'Nobody knows exactly. When you get up at five o'clock, pray nine times a day, work in the kitchen or the garden, read for half an hour and then go to bed after tea, there isn't much to say, really. In fact, talking with you like this is the first lengthy conversation *I've* had for a number of weeks. Since querying a greengrocer's bill.'

Somewhere, not far away, I heard the sound of a door banging. It made me jump.

'What's wrong?' she asked.

'I heard a noise,' I said. 'Sounded like a door banging in the wind.'

'Oh dear. That'll be the side entrance door! Matthew always forgets to close it!'

'Matthew?'

'The young man who sometimes helps with the heavy work in the yard. He's inclined to be a bit forgetful. His mind's always on that motorbike of his—Blue Streak—and never on his work. He dotes on that machine like a mother on a baby.' Sister Jerome sighed. 'I'd better go and lock the door.'

She vanished to go and close the door. I pulled out my phone and called Boges again.

Finally, he picked up.

'I spoke to Winter,' I said. 'Now before you get mad, just listen to what I have to say.'

'Go ahead,' he said, unsurprised.

'According to Winter, there's something written on the Jewel. Something revealing that concerns the Ormond Singularity.'

'She's dreaming. There's nothing written on it. We would have seen it by now if there was. Hang on while I get it.'

I waited until Boges returned. 'Like I said. There's nothing written on it. That girl is trouble. Why would you believe her?'

'Have you got a magnifying glass?' I remembered Dad taking a magnifying glass to his photos. 'Surely you have something like that lying around in your room?'

'Why?'

'Please just get one and go over the Jewel really carefully. All over. There might be something that we've missed. Winter also warned me that Sligo has a few leads on my location. I'm hoping no-one's on their way here.'

'You're at Redcliffe?'

'At Manresa *Convent*, can you believe it? Millicent's a nun! She goes by the name of Sister Mary Perpetua!'

Boges's deep laugh echoed down the line. 'Bet you didn't see that one coming!'

'I sure didn't, but it's no laughing matter—apparently she hasn't spoken for twenty years!'

I heard Boges exhale, frustrated, on the other end of the line, putting a quick end to his laughter.

'Somehow, I have to break through the wall of silence. Otherwise this trip will have been a waste of time.'

'What makes you think she'll speak to you?'

Sister Jerome wandered back into the kitchen.

'Gotta go, Boges. Promise me you'll go over the Jewel with a magnifying glass?'

'Why should I? Just because that sneaky girl, Winter, wants to hook you back onto the line?'

'Just do what I say. Please,' I said, then hung up.

'The side door was wide open!' said Sister Jerome, once I'd buried my phone back in my pocket. 'Anything could have blown in! Just as well your ears are sharp. I think that door needs attention. I don't think it's always Matthew's forgetfulness. I'll have to have a word to Sister Mary Bertha. She's the handyperson round here when we're left to our own devices. She's as strong as an ox!'

Sister Jerome hung the laundry key on a peg on the wall. Among the collection of keys beside it, I could see a set of car keys on a Saint Christopher key ring. The minibus, I thought. The nuns must have outings after all.

'I've also just spoken to Mother Superior about you,' Sister Jerome continued, 'and because of the weather and because you're the nephew of one of the sisters, she says she's happy for me to make up a bed for you.'

'What about seeing my aunt? I really need to speak to her. Even if she won't answer me.'

'Let's talk about it in the morning. It's getting rather late now. After evening prayers we go into the great silence. I shouldn't even be speaking now,' she said with a cheeky grin. 'Nobody speaks until after breakfast tomorrow.'

The great silence? Maybe that's where my great-aunt had learned her skill, I thought.

I followed Sister Jerome along several gloomy corridors lined with closed doors, until we came to a door halfway down a long hall. The nun opened it and I found myself in a small room with barred windows, a narrow bed, a table and chair, and a stone floor. I'd slept in a lot of strange places, but a convent? This was the eeriest yet.

'It's almost like a cell,' I said, before realising I probably sounded rude.

'It *is* a cell,' said Sister Jerome. 'And the nun who used to sleep here has gone to her reward.'

'Her reward?' I asked, confused.

'Yes. She's with the Lord now.'

So now I was sleeping in a dead nun's bed. It just got better and better!

'All the cells along this corridor used to be

filled with nuns, back in the old days. But the world has changed, even more than we realise, I expect, and this is the only empty cell still made up with furniture and bedding. There are extra blankets in a box under the bed.' She patted the end of the mattress and a thick cloud of dust lifted.

'I'll bid you goodnight then,' she said, clapping the dust from her hands. 'We get up at five o'clock so don't be alarmed if you hear people moving around in the dark.'

After she closed the door, I went to the window and peered through the bars, watching the rain slash against the glass. Compared to the warmth of the kitchen, this cell was cold. Outside the strong iron bars the wind was howling in the storm.

I should have felt safe but I didn't.

I kept my clothes on and crawled into the bed, thinking of my great-aunt—Sister Mary Perpetua—sleeping somewhere in this convent, lost in silence.

19 JULY

166 days to go . . .

Manresa Convent, Redcliffe

8:50 am

📱 cal. ok, ok, i'm sorry. winter was right. there is something written on the jewel! not sure what, yet, but it's in french.

📱 unreal! call u soon.

Sister Jerome fed me again in the large kitchen—porridge and toast. We had the place to ourselves, she told me. Apparently most of the nuns ate together shortly after dawn, then headed to the small chapel that was attached to the building for Morning Prayer.

9:26 am

The roar of a powerful motorbike made me jump as it pulled up outside.

'Ah,' said Sister Jerome, 'there's Matthew on Blue Streak, arriving for work. Perhaps you could give him a hand today? I'm sure he'd love the company of someone other than us nuns, for a change!'

'Sure,' I said, 'but can I see my aunt first?'

Sister Jerome patted my hand. 'Don't worry, dear, I'll see to it that you have your time with her. Just don't expect too much from it. Understood?'

10:05 am

I waited behind Sister Jerome as she knocked gently and then opened the door of a cell upstairs. I followed her in.

In a chair by the window, with a blanket over her knees, sat a very old nun, swathed in black robes and a veil, with a white band across her forehead. She had the waxy, pale skin of a woman who'd been cooped up inside for a long time.

Millicent.

As we walked towards her, she slowly turned in our direction. When her gaze moved from Sister Jerome to me, her face turned as grey as death.

She shuddered and gripped the arms of her chair with her bony old hands and attempted to stand up, stumbling and almost falling. Sister Jerome and I rushed forward to help steady her.

She pushed us both away and stepped back,

looking dumbfounded. Her voice came in a hoarse whisper.

'Barty?' she croaked. 'You've come to see me? Barty!' she repeated. 'My little brother!'

I heard a startled gasp from Sister Jerome. 'Mother of God, she spoke! Perpetua spoke!' She ran to the door, opened her mouth as if to call the other sisters, then must have thought better of it. She returned to the side of the stooped old nun. 'Perpetua, dear, you must sit down again. Here, let me help you.'

I took her other fragile arm and we supported her and guided her back into her chair.

Sister Jerome stared at me and tried to speak quietly into my ear, but her excitement was impossible to subdue. 'They are the first words she's spoken in over twenty years! This is remarkable!'

It *was* remarkable, but I wasn't Barty. And it made me sad knowing that I had to look into her hopeful eyes and let her down.

'I'm not Barty,' I finally said to my great-aunt as she searched the evidently familiar features of my face. 'He's my uncle. My *great*-uncle,' I added. 'I'm Cal, not Barty.'

'You must look like he did—when he was a boy,' Sister Jerome whispered to me. 'She's a tad confused.'

Again, my great-aunt tried to stand up, but this time her strength failed her and she fell right back into her chair.

'You mustn't tire yourself like this, Perpetua,' said Sister Jerome tenderly. 'We've all been wondering if we would ever hear your voice again. Praise the Lord. Speaking after twenty years. You've worked a miracle, young man,' she said to me, with a pat on my back. 'Now you two stay here, and I'll fetch us some warm drinks.'

I stood there looking at the old lady whose features reminded me of Great-uncle Bartholomew—without the bristles. Well, without *all* the bristles.

'Sister Mary Perpetua,' I started, sitting on the edge of the bed beside her. 'I'm afraid I'm not Barty. I'm your great-nephew, Callum Ormond. Tom's son and William's grandson.' I thought of William, the grandfather I'd hardly known. The family lost him shortly after I was born.

'I visited your brother Bartholomew recently,' I said, hoping it wasn't too early to be drilling her with questions. I didn't want to waste time, so I pressed on. 'He told me that you might have information about the Ormond family—about a will made by Piers Ormond. It's really important that I get hold of anything you might have. It's more important than anyone could imagine.'

She didn't move or speak for what seemed a long time, and I wondered whether she'd even heard what I'd said.

'I have been praying this moment would never come,' she finally spoke again, in a voice that cracked and scraped like a rusty gate. 'For a moment, I thought eighty years had slipped away and I was a girl again. Silly Milly,' she said with a hint of a childish smile.

'What do you mean, you've been praying this moment would never come?' I asked.

The hint of a smile disappeared and her lips tightened. She shook her head, remaining silent.

'Please, please tell me? What did you mean by that?'

I leaned forward as her rusty voice returned. 'Because it means that Billy's boy—your father . . .'

'Yes, please go on,' I begged. 'What about my father? Please tell me?'

It was just days away from the anniversary of Dad's death, and I had a queasy, sick feeling around my heart at the thought of him. I stared into Millicent's eyes, urging her soul to open up to me. Her silence almost made me feel like shaking it out of her—it was obvious there were many memories stirring inside. But when I saw that tears were now rolling down her pale, wrinkled cheeks, I calmed myself down.

'Please, Sister,' I said in the gentlest voice I could manage. 'What does my visit mean? What does it mean about my father?'

'It means,' she said in a voice so soft that I had to move closer to hear, 'it means that your father is dead.'

Her words floored me. How did she know that?

'He wrote to me, asking me about the Ormond Singularity,' she said.

I could hardly breathe.

Suddenly questions poured out of me as tension and exhilaration battled in my mind. 'And did you have any answers for him? Do you know anything? Can you tell me? Did he say what the Singularity was? Or what it was about? Please, it's crucial I find out.'

Outside the convent window, magpies were carolling.

'I left all family matters behind when I entered the convent,' she said. 'All the papers, all the information on the Ormond Singularity, were put away. In a big envelope.' The old woman took a deep breath. 'I couldn't help him. I only remembered it being spoken about it when I was a girl.'

'Do you remember what was said about the Ormond Singularity?'

'Only that it was a secret kept in our family—

a *deadly* secret. It has been the death of all of the Ormonds who have tried to unravel it. It should remain a secret.'

I shivered. *It killed your father. It'll kill you,* the staggering man had warned me on New Year's Eve.

'And that's how I knew he must be dead,' she continued. 'Because anyone who starts to investigate the Ormond Singularity . . . winds up in a casket . . .' My great-aunt's voice trailed off and she stared silently out into the distance through the window near her chair.

So many people wanted me dead. I knew that already. But was she saying the Ormond Singularity killed Dad?

I waited a moment before changing tack. 'Do you have any information about a relative of ours—Piers Ormond?'

'Our family is full of secrets,' she whispered, 'and the Ormond Singularity is the deadliest secret of all. My grandfather, may he rest in peace, warned me of that.' She stopped for a moment. 'Piers was an uncle of mine. He gathered a lot of information about the Ormond family.'

'Do you know anything about his will?'

I took one of her frail hands in mine, but her glazed eyes showed her attention had drifted away again.

'Sister, do you know anything about what the Ormond Singularity is?' I was still hopeful my questioning might stir up old memories, old files, stored deep in her mind.

'Come closer, nephew,' she beckoned. I shuffled in, heart racing. Did she have some information after all? 'The Ormond Singularity is the great secret of the Ormonds.'

'But what *is* it?' I persisted.

'Did Bartholomew send you?'

'Yes,' I said, awkwardly, not wanting to have to tell her that the lethal Ormond secret had killed him too. I recalled the old man lying on the floor as the flames raced through his house. 'He told me you were like the family historian and that you looked after all the family papers and documents, including information about Piers Ormond's will.'

'Do you know we're twins?' she said with a smile, dismissing what I'd just said. 'Bartholomew and I.'

'*Twins?*' I asked, surprised.

Her smile quickly transformed into something much more serious and fearful.

'I heard,' she said, nodding, and looking deep into my eyes, 'about the two babies. Something terrible happened.'

The newspaper clipping—had it been about

them? Bartholomew and Millicent? It had looked old, but not *that* old, and I'd been feeling more and more like it had something to do with *me*.

'Who were those babies?' I asked. 'They were twins—you and Barty?' I suggested. 'What happened to them?'

She shook her head slowly, but I wasn't sure whether it was in response to my question, or a reaction to the memory.

The old nun started weeping, and then in a quavery voice she started singing.

'*Two little lambs in the cold night frost, one was saved and the other one lost.*'

The song unnerved me. It was haunting, and somehow familiar, even though I'd never heard it before. Almost as quickly as she'd started singing, my great-aunt stopped, looking at me in a puzzled way.

'Tell me, again. Why are you here?'

I was frustrated, confused, spooked. For the moment, I had to leave the mystery of the abducted babies behind and concentrate on why I had come.

'I hoped you had important family documents,' I reminded Sister Mary Perpetua, 'that could help me. You said there was an envelope?'

'All of my things have been put away,' she said. 'I don't remember where they are. But why would a youngster like you be interested in the affairs of an old woman like me?'

The brightness in her face faded. It seemed she'd forgotten pieces of our conversation. Her eyes clouded and she slowly started muttering the song again, caught up in another world.

'*Two little lambs in the cold night frost, one was saved and the other one lost,*' she repeated in her crackly voice. 'That's how it was,' she said, turning back to me. Tears were falling gently down her face. 'One was returned safely, the other one was lost. Gone. We leave our worldly life behind us when we come into the convent,' she said in a different voice, as if she were quoting someone else's words.

Sister Jerome returned with a tray of sandwiches and hot chocolate for both of us. She put them down on a small table by the wall and sat down beside me. I was edgy, restless, eager to find out where the family papers had been stored.

I tried again. 'Sister Mary Perpetua, where did you store everything? The family documents?'

She ignored me, focusing on humming her strange, sad song. She stared out the window once more. I turned to Sister Jerome. Her kindly face was creased with anxiety. She shrugged her shoulders as if to say: sorry, I can't help you.

'Please, Sister Mary Perpetua, tell me.'

But it was no use. As suddenly as her voice had returned it had left again. She had closed down. She ignored the tray Sister Jerome had brought in and sat slumped in her chair, as though she'd used up the last of her energy in the burst of cryptic words that had broken her twenty-year retreat.

I'd spent days on the road, pinning my hopes on finding Bartholomew's sister, Millicent. And now I had found her, and she had confirmed the danger that I knew surrounded the Ormond Singularity, but the rest of the information I needed was trapped in her befuddled mind.

'She put everything away,' I said to Sister Jerome as she ushered me towards the door. 'She said something about a big envelope.'

Sister Jerome smoothed out her robes, and grinned. 'I think I know where it is!'

11:22 am

We left my great-aunt behind, humming away, and Sister Jerome hurried me downstairs.

'Where are we going?'

From a fold in her robe, Sister Jerome drew a ring of old-fashioned keys. 'To the archives!'

She led me to a door at the end of a corridor. I waited while she unlocked it, stepped in and switched on a light. We were faced with a creepy opening in the floor—a flight of stone stairs descending into the darkness of a cellar.

'All the convent's archives are kept down here,' she said, as I followed her down the narrow steps.

At the bottom, Sister Jerome switched on another light. We were in a cold, damp underground room, a little bigger than Repro's place, lined with shelves and cabinets. Unlike Repro's place, these shelves were orderly and neat, arranged meticulously with bulging folders and files from the ground to the ceiling. In an alcove down the far end were two large wooden chests, one on top of the other.

'The oldest archives are kept in here,' said Sister Jerome, blowing dust off the top chest. 'Unfortunately, the earliest records will be right down there in that bottom chest. Sister Mary Perpetua's been with us for nearly seventy years. Twice as long as me. Please give me a hand to lift these off so that we can get to it.' She stepped back for a moment, her hands on her hips. 'I still can't believe she spoke!' she said. 'She must have been waiting for just the right moment! Or just the right person!'

With renewed energy, we lifted the top chest down onto the floor, freeing up the lower one.

I felt a thrill as Sister Jerome unlocked and

lifted its creaking lid. It was filled with dusty packets and folders tied up with pink tape. She rummaged around, sorting through the packets until she came to a thick, dark-brown envelope.

'Here it is!' Sister Jerome handed it to me. 'I knew it would be here.'

The flowery, old-fashioned handwriting on the front of it read: 'Millicent Butler Ormond, 1939.'

12:02 pm

A cold wind blew in from outside and I snatched my hoodie from where it had been hanging out to dry.

Back in my room I opened the envelope and emptied it on the bed. Sister Jerome had suggested I stay another night—she thought it was worth taking my time going through the documents—and then trying to speak to my great-aunt again in the morning, after she'd had a good rest. Even though I was worried about Sligo searching for me here, I was quick to accept the offer—I felt like my great-aunt had so much more she could tell me, if I persisted. I wanted to find out everything I could from her. I was convinced she could shed light on some of the darkness that engulfed our family.

In front of me were three letters from Piers Ormond, sent back to his family during

his travels, and a very sketchy family tree with
some familiar names, and some areas that were
faded and stained.

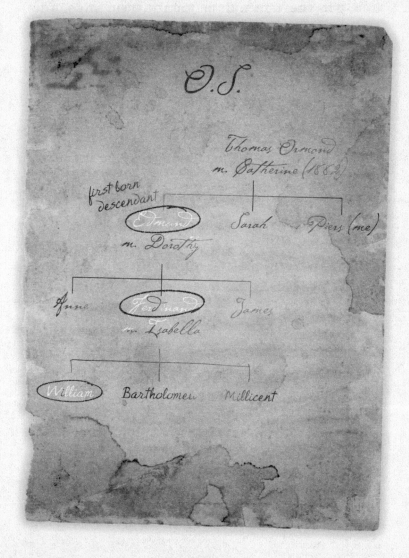

I had thought Bartholomew was older than my grandfather but, of course, William was the first-born.

I put the incomplete family tree aside and skimmed through the letters. The words 'Ormond Angel' and 'Ormond Riddle' immediately jumped to my attention. Piers Ormond knew about the Angel and the Riddle! I couldn't wait to tell Boges and go over them with him!

Just when I was about to settle down and read them all properly, someone knocked on my door.

'Yes?'

'Hi, I'm Matt. Sister Jerome said you could help me out with some yard work this afternoon?'

'Sure,' I reluctantly agreed, putting everything aside and getting up to join him. I'd have to look at it all again later.

20 JULY

165 days to go . . .

4:28 am

I lay in the narrow bed, listening hard. The rain that had returned overnight had stopped, and trees shook outside the window, casting soft shadows in my room. The silence of the convent was so deep, yet something had woken me from my sleep.

It was too early, even for the nuns. I got out of bed and put my ear to the door.

The noise had faded, but I quietly stepped out of my room and peered up and down the corridor. Its gloomy length was empty. At one end, a T-junction, a red lamp flickered in front of a statue.

There it was again!

The sound seemed to be coming from the left-hand side of the T-junction.

My bare feet made no sound as I crept down the corridor towards the flickering light.

As I approached the corner, I heard it again.

I froze, pressing myself flat against the wall, listening. It was the sound of someone opening and closing doors, softly, stealthily. Maybe one of them had slammed unexpectedly. Someone was creeping around, searching . . .

The pattern repeated—the footsteps continued, paused, and then came the sound of a door being opened. I imagined the person listening for a few moments outside the door, then opening it, checking that the room was empty, closing the door and stepping quietly to the next one.

The footsteps were getting closer. I waited till I heard the sound of another door opening, and risked a peek around the corner.

I jumped back. I saw the figure of a very tall nun whose height cut her habit short above her ankles. Was it Sister Bertha checking the locks at this hour? She must have been crazy. Or an insomniac.

'Sister Bertha?' I asked as she moved to test the next door.

She swung round to face me.

My body jolted with fear as the face came into focus—it wasn't Sister Bertha! It wasn't Sister anyone! It was Zombrovski, rigged out in a nun's habit!

He was as shocked as I was, but I was faster! I skidded away in the opposite direction, slipping and sliding on the floorboards, racing down the corridor.

Zombie looked like the most evil sister in the world! He must have been chasing me using one of Sligo's leads—my great-aunt!

I retreated through the building the way I'd come with Sister Jerome, running silently on bare feet to the other end of the corridor, way past my room, and then around another corner. I waited, holding my breath, occasionally sneaking a fast look behind me.

I jumped back again. He was standing at the far end of the corridor I had just raced down, and seemed to be sniffing the air and listening for noise.

What if he went into my room and grabbed my backpack? I was so relieved I'd handed most of my things over to Boges to care for, but I didn't want to lose all of the archive papers I'd just got my hands on. But Zombie didn't seem interested in my belongings right now. He was only interested in getting me.

My pulse was racing. I had to come up with a plan to deal with this. There was no way to get past him. If I could just get out the front door and lose myself in the darkness, Zombie could think I'd fled the convent.

I was torn between running away and trying

to get back to my cell, and my backpack. Zombie's heavy, relentless footsteps neared and that made the decision for me. There was no time to collect my stuff, I had to get out. I ran in silence into the gloomy foyer. As I braced myself to charge through the front doors, a candle in front of the armoured saint suddenly flared up in a burst of radiance, illuminating the silver sword. I stopped and stared at it for a second.

What if Zombie wasn't alone? What if someone was waiting for me outside, waiting for me to run right into them?

Fight or flight? I had to decide!

Fight! I shot over to the Saint Ignatius statue and wrenched the sword from its position, easily snapping the rusty wire that held it in place. It wasn't sharp, but would make a strong impact. I positioned myself behind the wall to the side of the corridor opening, the sword raised high above my head.

I waited, holding my breath in tense silence as Zombie came closer and closer. Any second now and he'd emerge from the darkness of the corridor. And I'd be ready.

Zombie appeared out of the gloom, and I lifted the sword higher. He sensed my presence and jerked his head in my direction. In the glow of the fading candlelight, the rage in his eyes burned brightly.

He snarled and hurled himself at me, not seeing the sword I held above my head. I brought it down as hard as I could across his shoulders as he twisted, sending him flying against the wall. He sprawled, hands out, and that's when I saw the knuckleduster on his right hand! Four heavy points of metal decorated his fist. I hesitated—I didn't want to *kill* him, but I didn't want to be killed either! Cursing with fury, he staggered back to his feet.

Terror shuddered through me, energising my fight. Sligo didn't want me reaching my sixteenth birthday, but I wasn't about to let him get his way!

I raised the sword again as Zombie came at me, literally ripping the black fabric of the nun's habit off his body. This time I was really going to let him have it. I had no other option. But as I swung the sword, I skidded on a pool of water blown under the front door by the storm, and fell hard on the coil of the bell tower rope. The sword flew out of my hand and as I scrambled and grabbed it again, my left foot tripped on the rope.

The shocking, booming sound of the bell ringing above startled us both. As Zombie squared up again to take me down with a blow of his metal fist, I jumped backwards, swinging the sword with both hands. He was stronger but slower than me and as he lashed out with the knuckleduster, I smashed the sword down hard on his right shoulder. He roared in pain and folded to his knees, howling.

I still hadn't stopped him—I'd just enraged him even more! He staggered to his feet, switching the knuckleduster over to his other fist.

I stepped back, flattening myself against the railing of the bell tower staircase. I ducked a deadly left-handed punch, and jumped sideways, hearing the splintering sound of Zombie's fist crunching into the timber of the stairs. His arm was tightly wedged in the broken wood, giving me a second to move.

I had nowhere to go but up.

With a roar he freed himself and came after me again, one arm hanging uselessly from his shoulder. I charged up the stairs. The bell ropes that dangled down the centre of the spiral staircase slapped around us, keeping the bell ringing as we bumped and bashed our way along.

Zombie suddenly lurched and grabbed at my ankle. I turned and deflected the swinging knuckleduster with a slice of the sword. It clanged on connection, and the jarring force behind Zombie's attack sent the sword flying out of my grip.

It clattered to a standstill a few steps higher. Zombie was closing in on me. The bell rang louder and louder in my ears and I started panicking, not having a clue what I was going to do when we both reached the top of the tower. I took the stairs backwards, afraid to take my eyes off him, my fingers scrabbling around blindly behind me, trying to locate the sword.

Finally I snatched it up and ran faster up the staircase, twisting and turning higher and higher.

Zombie charged after me, cursing, close behind.

I made it to the top of the stairs and the big belfry where the giant bell vibrated in a square tower with tall, wide stone arches on each side. The bell, still trembling and humming from when it had rung moments earlier, took up most of the room with only a narrow walkway round it. There was nowhere to go, nowhere to hide— there was only the black night and the ground, a long, long way down. Wind blew in mercilessly through the open arches, grazing the bell, as I realised the death sentence I'd given myself . . . I was completely snookered.

I shivered, grasping the sword tightly, waiting for Zombie to strike.

He appeared at the top of the staircase, and

in the dim moonlight his evil, menacing smirk tore into me. Zombie knew he had me trapped. The only way was down and he had the stairwell opening covered.

Through gritted teeth, he seemed to laugh. Leaning back into one of the open arches, he propped himself up on the stone edging. Next he grabbed onto the ornate railing that ran around the very top of the tower, where the points of the arches met. He lifted himself up like he was co-ordinating a pro-wrestling manoeuvre. It took me a couple of seconds to work out exactly what he was doing—he was setting himself up to plough maximum pressure on the bell, swinging it wildly with the force of both of his feet. I was trapped and he was going to crush me against the wall with the huge bell!

He grinned, seeing the fear on my face.

'Goodbye, Cal,' he grunted, then lifted his weight and gave the bell an almighty shove with his powerful legs.

The massive bell swung fast towards me. I swerved, following Zombie's lead by leaping up, grabbing onto the railing above me and swinging my body out to avoid the killer collision. Air rushed as the huge bell scraped my body, its full force missing me by mere millimetres. The colossal structure bashed hard against the wall, its chime distorted by the masonry it struck instead of me. The return swing of the bell, fuelled by immense rebound momentum, swept back in the path of its unsuspecting victim—Zombie.

He was perched precariously on the arch edge, and the swinging bell caught him off balance, slamming into him, sending him reeling backwards! His face was white with horror as he flew straight through the open arch, freefalling into the night.

His screams pierced through the air, ending with an unbelievable thud.

I didn't know whether to yell with triumph or cringe at Zombie's horrific plunge. All I knew was that I had to dodge the bell as I cautiously peered over the edge of the arch he'd tumbled through.

Below, I could just make out his body lying still, caught on the serrated arms of the cactus. It didn't look good.

I bolted down the bell tower stairs, carrying the warrior sword by my side.

Sister Jerome ran towards me in a long white nightgown and a frilly cap, just like she'd stepped out of an old movie. She had a furious look on her face.

'What on earth do you think you're doing, young man?'

Someone flicked a switch and light filled the room. Close behind Sister Jerome was a group of nuns in matching nighties and caps, each of them armed with mops, candlesticks and garden tools.

'Explain yourself this minute!'

I leaned the sword against the wall and stepped down to join her.

'There was an intruder,' I said, 'dressed up like a nun. I think he was trying to steal from one of the rooms when I caught him,' I said, thinking fast. 'He attacked me, chased me up the bell tower.'

'I thought my pocket watch was missing!' cried one of the nuns.

Suddenly, my legs felt like they were made of jelly. I leaned against the stair that Zombie had splintered with his fist.

'Well, where is he now?' she asked, nervously looking around.

'He fell.'

'What do you mean, he fell?' Sister Jerome questioned me.

'He fell through one of the arches.' I pointed up, to indicate the bell tower.

'Holy Mary, Mother of God,' whispered Sister Jerome, her face aghast. 'Come on,' she said as she ushered the nuns around her. 'We'd better go see how he is.'

The flock of nuns shuffled to the double doors of the convent and opened them, carrying with them orbs of candlelight. Once outside, it was easy to spot where Zombie had landed. I couldn't see his body, but there was a deep indent in the silhouettes of the cactuses, where his weight had crushed the plants beneath him. As the candlelight shifted, I saw one of his hands, hanging twisted, bloody and lifeless.

Sister Jerome clambered up to him with another nun close by. They crouched down in the garden while I stood back. From where I was standing, the tower looked crazy-tall. It rose up right into the sky. Taking a tumble from that height would have been . . .

Sister Jerome gasped.

The nun beside her stood up and turned to us, her face mortified.

'He's dead,' she whispered.

5:58 am

Zombrovski had broken his neck in the fall. I watched in complete shock as everyone huddled around him, whispering prayers and rubbing tiny silver crosses.

The nuns found the missing pocket watch, some rosary beads, and a ring in Zombrovski's pocket. Luckily for me, the big crim couldn't resist an opportunity to steal from sleeping nuns, even when he was stalking the halls, searching for me.

'Are you all right, Cal?' asked Sister Jerome as someone draped a bed sheet over Zombie's body. I'd been standing alone, in the doorway, trying to take in all of what had just happened. 'He didn't hurt you, did he?'

'No, I'm fine, thanks. Just feel a bit shocked,' I explained, showing her my shaking legs.

'You used that?' she asked, pointing to the sword in the foyer that I'd taken from the Saint Ignatius statue.

I nodded. 'To protect myself, yes.'

'You did very well. Saint Ignatius was a warrior. I'm sure he'd be proud of you. That poor chap looks like he was a nasty piece of work,' she said, staring back again at the shape lying in the garden under the sheet. 'I bet he never expected his night of looting would turn out like that.' She shook her head and tut-tutted her tongue before starting to fuss over the bruises and cuts I'd received, courtesy of Zombie. 'It's a strange business,' she said, pausing to examine my skinned hands, 'getting an intruder not long after your arrival. We were very lucky you were here.'

A tall nun with an air of authority approached

us. 'Sister Jerome,' she said while tying her nightcap more securely around her plump face, 'could you please notify the authorities? Advise them of the intruder, the thefts, and his death.'

'Certainly, Mother Superior,' obliged Sister Jerome.

The police would be on their way in minutes, and I didn't want to think about how Sligo was going to react now that one of his men was out of action. Permanently. I needed to get out of Manresa. I needed to get out of Redcliffe.

'You were very brave—and *foolish*,' said Sister Jerome. 'I'll certainly mention your courage to Sergeant McInerney when he arrives. He will want to have a word with you, I'm sure. I'd best get inside and phone him.'

6:21 am

Sister Jerome was on the phone speaking with the police, which meant it was time for me to get as far away from Zombrovski's body as possible. I knew I only had minutes to get out, so I raced down the hall to my room.

I collected up all of my things, and then stuffed them, plus the new papers from the convent archive, into my backpack. I slung it over my shoulders, bolted out of the room and skidded down the corridor again. I had to leave Millicent behind, and hope that the documents would give me enough clues to keep going.

Near the convent entrance, I heard a couple of cars pull up. The nuns that had been milling around the foyer rushed to the door to see who'd arrived.

'That'll be Sergeant McInerney,' said Sister Jerome, pulling a black cloak around her. I tried to look casual and conceal the bag on my back. 'Come along, Cal,' she said. 'Let's go talk to him.'

'You go ahead,' I called. 'I just have to duck into the bathroom first.'

I waited until she'd walked outside before I dashed across the kitchen towards the back exit near the laundry. I could hear Sister Jerome and Mother Superior talking to the officers. Their voices were getting louder and I figured they must have been on their way in. I took off through the back door, flew past the laundry, and over the vegetable patch and herb gardens, around to the side of the convent.

I peered out from behind the wall, assessing who I had to get past in the front grounds. The sun was just starting to come up, sending soft light over the police car and coroner's van that were parked on the grass to the side of the drive-way. A group was huddled around Zombrovski's body, which was still sprawled out on top of the crushed cactus plants. Cameras flashed and nuns muttered amongst themselves.

I didn't think my feet could carry me away fast enough down the driveway, through the gates and away from the big Manresa property. I looked around the backyard for ideas. The mini-bus flashed into my mind, but I couldn't possibly go back inside to retrieve the keys. Not now.

As if in answer to my prayers, standing near the shed, the key still in the ignition, was an awesome, custom-decorated motorbike. Glossy blue, its streamlined curves and chrome-plated engine fittings, together with silver, curved knives joining the wheels to the hub instead of spokes, created a gleaming machine just asking to be ridden. This had to be Blue Streak, the motorbike belonging to Matt, the guy I'd helped in the garden yesterday.

He was standing next to one of the cops who was looming over the body taking notes. They both had their backs to me.

Boges and I had ridden trail bikes a few times with another guy from school a couple of years ago, but I'd never been on anything like this blue monster! I jumped onto the heavy bike, bouncing into the saddle, one leg on the ground to steady myself. I made sure my backpack was on tight and pulled the sleek, black helmet that hung from the handlebars over my head. I switched on the ignition, jumped on the accelerator, and kicked away the stand. I scooted my leg along the ground, helping the bike move, while turning the throttle under my hand. The powerful bike roared into acceleration and I was off, heading for the gates.

Before I had even reached the front yard, a gunshot rang out—a bullet whizzed past me! I hunched over the bike—I couldn't believe it! The police were shooting at me!

How did they know who I was?

I wrenched the bike to the left, skidding wildly as I aimed for the back of the shed, ducking under a line of washing on my way. Within seconds, voices were shouting and people were scrambling.

My chest was pounding as I turned the bike around and peered out from behind the cover of the shed and through the washing. I scanned the whole area, searching for the shooter.

It was when my eyes were drawn up high that I caught a glimpse of my sinister assailant.

It wasn't the police who had fired at me . . . it was Bruno—*Red Singlet!*

He was hunched over one of the bell tower arches, the perfect 360-degree position for a sniper. A sniper with a vengeance.

Now I was really scared.

Another shot ricocheted off an incinerator and splintered through the shed wall, just centimetres from where I was keeping watch. Didn't he realise the police were already here?

The shouting surrounding the convent had intensified and sirens were approaching. Sergeant McInerney must have called for backup the second he heard the first shot ring out. I could sense people stirring, and preparing for an attack, but I couldn't take my eyes off Bruno.

The once peaceful convent was now hosting the cops, a dead body, Bruno—Sligo's top man— *and* the most wanted juvenile in the state. I was in double danger—I had to dodge Bruno *and* the police, and somehow make a desperate rush on the motorbike, in full view, out the gates.

I had to break cover and go for it. There was no other way. I couldn't wait for them to come and get me. I silently walked the bike along to the edge of the shed closest to the gate, a leg on each side of the engine housing. My plan was to kick the accelerator, grit my teeth and fly behind the line of washing, then weave my way out.

Even with the police presence increasing by the second, Bruno could still fire off the shot that would ensure I never reached my sixteenth birthday.

7:01 am

Police were yelling through a loudspeaker now, ordering Bruno to put down his weapon, and aiming their pistols up at the bell tower. If their attention stayed on him, maybe I would live after all.

I pictured what I had to do—gunning the bike and getting the hell out of there through the gates! But then I saw something I hadn't accounted for. Two police officers, weapons drawn, had positioned themselves on either side of the gates, on the dirt road.

I would have to ride straight past them. There was no way I could do that without being seen. My brain raced feverishly, trying to formulate an idea.

More gunshots rang out. I jumped back as one bullet darted past my head, while a second bullet hit one of the squad car windscreens, shattering it. I heard a police vehicle screech around the back of the convent, adding to the force already in place, blocking Bruno's escape—and mine. I could feel the sweat breaking out on my face as I switched on the ignition. Blue Streak roared into action.

I released the brake and pushed away, twisting the throttle full on. Blue Streak reared up and roared forward, jerking me with it. I clung on, squeezing my knees hard against it, keeping my balance as together we swerved fast towards the open gates.

The cops that were focused on the bell tower spun around to see what was going on. They recklessly turned their weapons to me, and shouted at me to stop.

No way!

A shot from the bell tower fired down at me, and the cops instantly turned their weapons back on Bruno. They didn't know who to aim for!

Taking advantage of their confusion I gunned the throttle and hunched over, riding like a speedway champion. I hurtled through the crossfire, through the gates, and along the dirt road, blowing the weeds and dust up behind me.

I'd made it out, unharmed. I clung on to the powerfully-charged motor, racing through the countryside, leaving Bruno behind to fight it out with the cops.

8:11 am

I kept riding, heading south, waiting for the sound of a siren to come up behind me. But it never came.

It wouldn't have taken long for the police to work out who I was—the Manresa guest who'd not-so-coincidentally arrived just before Zombrovski.

Blue Streak was a liability—cops would be alert and equipped with the vehicle's description at all surrounding locations—so I knew I was going to have to abandon it pretty soon. My plan was to ride as far as the fuel would take me, and then it'd be time to tackle my journey back to the city on foot.

When Blue Streak started shuddering with an emptied tank, I wheeled it into a sheltered spot off the road, covering it with branches and leaves. I hoped Matt would get over the fact that I'd taken his bike, and I hoped that it would be returned to him somehow. One day, I thought, I'd find a way to repay him.

24 JULY
161 days to go . . .

5 Enid Parade, Crystal Beach

2:02 am

📱 i'm back at enid. zombie's DEAD. crazy shootout with cops and bruno. don't know how i'm still alive. call me when u wake up.

Back on the rug in the living room, I looked through the three Piers Ormond letters. It wasn't just the spidery, fading sepia ink that made them difficult to read—once Piers finished writing a page, he'd turned the paper sideways and continued writing over the existing words. It was like he'd run out of paper or something.

I was falling asleep, but really wanted to get up and change my look. There were people gunning for me and I wasn't going to make it easy for them. The panic that pumped through my veins every day was pumping harder now that Zombie was dead. Yeah, it was one less guy chasing me, but now Sligo would be chasing me twice as hard.

I needed to look like another person. I stared at my reflection in the pristine, marble bathroom, then tore open a packet of brown dye I'd bought from a chemist, and fumbled around for a pair of scissors.

When I was done, my hair was darker, shorter, different. I scrubbed the sink, removing all remnants of hair and colour. Would the day ever come when I could just be myself?

7:21 am

'Zombrovski's dead?' Boges's voice came down the line, sleepy, but shocked. His call had woken me up, so I was just as dazed.

'He was trying to kill me,' I explained. 'I found him roaming the halls on my second night at the convent, and we fought each other all the way up this bell tower . . . and then when he was trying to wipe me out with this massive shove of the bell, I dodged it, and it ended up swinging back and swatting him out into the sky.'

Boges was silent, in what must have been disbelief.

'Broke his neck when he landed,' I added. 'The cops were on their way, so I knew I had to get out, but then Bruno showed up, guns blazing, so I had even more reason to get outta there.'

'Cal, that is not good news,' said Boges, very

seriously. 'Sligo will go even crazier trying to . . . to *get* you now.'

It was obvious Boges was trying to avoid saying *kill* you.

'I know,' I agreed. 'So I'm back at Enid Parade. Your uncle's not going to spring me here, is he?'

'Nah, you're cool there for now.'

'So tell me about what the Jewel says. What did you find?'

'I did what you said, and gave it the once-over with a powerful magnifying glass. At first, I thought the words were just tiny scratches, but when I looked really closely on the narrow strip of gold that runs around the inside, framing the portrait, I could see there were letters engraved near the hinges.'

'Say it: "Winter Frey was telling the truth".'

Boges groaned.

'Go on.'

Boges groaned again. Louder.

'Go on!'

'All right, all right, she was telling the truth!' he admitted. 'But don't think that means I trust her all of a sudden. Anyway, back to business: it's in French. I've run it through an online translator, but it's turned up all sorts of rubbish.'

'All we need to do then is find someone who speaks French,' I said, instantly thinking of

Winter—she seemed like the type of girl who'd understand French. 'And we need to take a look at these letters I took from the convent archive.'

'Did you find Piers Ormond's will?'

'No, but I have some old letters of his. They're really hard to read,' I added.

'So, what are we waiting for? Let's meet up already,' said Boges. 'I'll come over as soon as I can.'

'How's your back fence escape route?' I asked. 'You sure it's safe?'

'Should be OK. I won't come if it's not. No-one's been out on the street for days. And Zombrovski was the regular house-sitter, but I guess he won't be coming round any time soon.' Boges laughed awkwardly. 'This arvo cool?'

'Yep. See you when you get here.'

4:32 pm

'Nice look!' said Boges, in a way that made me unsure whether he was making fun of me or not. My hair was pretty different, and I was wearing a blazer I'd picked up at a thrift store, over jeans and a T-shirt.

'Something smells good. What's in the bag?' I asked, checking out the heavy-duty bag Boges had in tow.

He looked down at his watch. 'Early dinner?'

We tucked into some kebabs, and in between

greedy mouthfuls I gave Boges a more detailed run-down of my trip to Manresa, Redcliffe. When we'd finished we took a look at the Jewel.

'It never leaves my side,' said Boges, carefully handing it to me, along with a magnifying glass. 'Take a look for yourself.'

Sure enough, what had looked like nothing but tiny scratches before suddenly jumped into focus, and groups of letters began forming words.

Boges held out a piece of paper. 'Here, I wrote it down.'

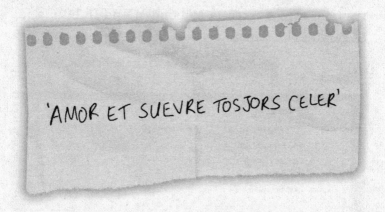

'AMOR ET SUEVRE TOSJORS CELER'

'Awesome,' I said. 'Something about celery!'

'"Amor" means "love",' Boges explained, 'but I'm not sure about the rest. I can ask Madame Rodini at school. I'll just tell her it's for a . . . umm . . . oh, I'll come up with something, don't worry. Your turn; let's take a look at the Piers Ormond letters.'

'Paper must have been scarce or something,' I said as I grabbed the envelope. 'Check it out; when he finished going one way, he turned the paper around and wrote over the top of what he'd just written.'

Boges pulled out his laptop, and handed the letters back to me. 'Start reading out loud and I'll type it up,' he said. 'That'll make it a bit easier. Just focus on following the lines.'

I put aside the first two, which were about travels from Australia to London and Dublin, and began on the third.

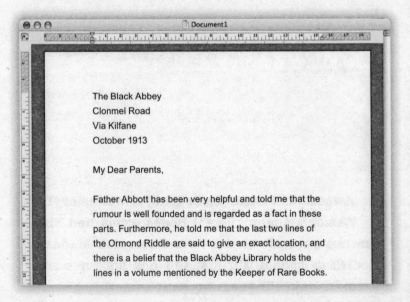

The Black Abbey
Clonmel Road
Via Kilfane
October 1913

My Dear Parents,

Father Abbott has been very helpful and told me that the rumour Is well founded and is regarded as a fact in these parts. Furthermore, he told me that the last two lines of the Ormond Riddle are said to give an exact location, and there is a belief that the Black Abbey Library holds the lines in a volume mentioned by the Keeper of Rare Books.

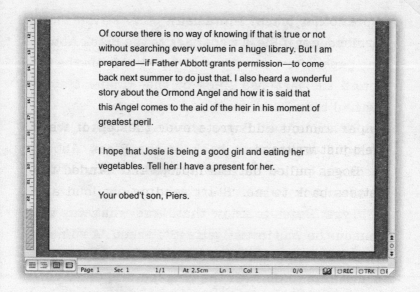

Of course there is no way of knowing if that is true or not without searching every volume in a huge library. But I am prepared—if Father Abbott grants permission—to come back next summer to do just that. I also heard a wonderful story about the Ormond Angel and how it is said that this Angel comes to the aid of the heir in his moment of greatest peril.

I hope that Josie is being a good girl and eating her vegetables. Tell her I have a present for her.

Your obed't son, Piers.

Page 1   Sec 1   1/1   At 2.5cm   Ln 1   Col 1   0/0   ○REC ○TRK ○E

'"Kilfane",' said Boges. 'That's from the transparency!'

'Yep,' I said, 'it was the first thing that jumped out at me.'

Boges dug through his backpack and brought out a folder with the transparency safely stashed in it. Sure enough there were the two names—G'managh and Kilfane, with the black dot between them. I remembered my kidnappers' interrogation: *Your father gave you a map. Where is it?*

Was this a map? Was this what they had been referring to?

'What do you think that black spot between them means?' I asked Boges.

'Another place? Unnamed?'

'I wonder if Piers went back to the Black Abbey the year after, like he said he would. Maybe he found the last two lines of the Riddle. Maybe he had them!'

'No, dude,' said Boges, shaking his head, 'Piers Ormond never went back to the Black Abbey. Because before he could, the First World War broke out in 1914.'

Trust Boges to know that. 'And what was the rumour he was investigating?' I asked. 'A rumour that was regarded as fact? Do you think it was something to do with the Ormond Singularity?'

Boges shrugged. 'I'm more interested in the fact that he believed there was a version of the complete Ormond Riddle in a book in the library at the Black Abbey. Or at least the last two lines.'

'Let's just jump on a bus and check out the Black Abbey library ourselves,' I joked.

Boges ran his hands through his hair. 'It's frustrating these places are so far away, but it's good to know that the Ormond Angel comes to the aid of the heir,' he said.

'I haven't noticed any angelic aid lately.'

'You're alive, aren't you?' Boges tapped his fingers impatiently over his laptop keyboard. 'Let's keep going.'

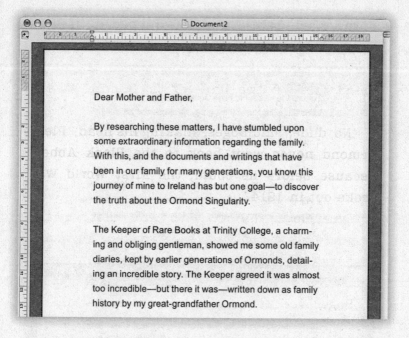

Dear Mother and Father,

By researching these matters, I have stumbled upon some extraordinary information regarding the family. With this, and the documents and writings that have been in our family for many generations, you know this journey of mine to Ireland has but one goal—to discover the truth about the Ormond Singularity.

The Keeper of Rare Books at Trinity College, a charming and obliging gentleman, showed me some old family diaries, kept by earlier generations of Ormonds, detailing an incredible story. The Keeper agreed it was almost too incredible—but there it was—written down as family history by my great-grandfather Ormond.

'Awesome! Piers Ormond was on the track all right!' said Boges. 'He knew way back then in 1913 about the Ormond Singularity. He was doing what we're doing! Trying to gather information and work it out.'

'And what Dad was doing nearly a century later,' I added. 'He'd also stumbled upon some incredible information that he didn't want to put down in writing. He was going to tell me all about it as soon as he got home. But by then he was too sick to tell me anything. Anything other than the cryptic messages in his drawings.'

'Sounds like we're talking late 1700s,' said

Boges, staring at the words he'd typed up, 'if Piers Ormond's great-grandfather was involved.'

I swore the Keeper of Rare Books to secrecy, in case it all turns out to be true. I think I may have offended him with that request, but he said that he was a loyal subject of the Crown and the keeper of many family secrets as well as medieval books. He described himself as a man of discretion.

On speaking with an antiquarian in a Dublin establishment, I also discovered that the last two lines were added onto the body of the existing Ormond Riddle manuscript at a later

date—sometime in the late sixteenth century. These two lines are not considered to be part of the original Riddle which dates from an earlier period—possibly circa 1550. Perhaps this is why they were removed? The antiquarian, O'Donnell and Sons, had no information as to what they contained; however, my thorough search of the Black Abbey Library next summer may finally reveal their missing message.

Perhaps the monks at the Black Abbey can tell me more, as I promise to tell you more when I arrive home. This is too important and too enormous to allow a whisper of it to get out. If I find any more information from the monks, I will leave it with my solicitor for safekeeping. I will be travelling to Carrick-on-Suir in the next few days.

Your dutiful and obed't son, Piers.

Boges looked up from his laptop, his round eyes wide with excitement. 'We are definitely getting closer to cracking the Dangerous Mystery of the Ormonds. This is awesome!'

'It would be more awesome,' I said, kicking myself, 'if I could remember the name of that solicitor. His firm could still be holding valuable information about my family and the Ormond Singularity.'

Boges gathered up the letters and carefully refolded them, squeezing the old envelope to make room to put them back in. Suddenly he frowned. 'What's this? There's something else in here.'

He tipped the envelope and shook it. A fine piece of paper fluttered out. I picked it up gently. 'It's an incomplete family tree,' I said, smoothing it down on the floor in front of us, 'in connection with the Ormond Singularity—I'm guessing that's what the initials "O.S." stand for.'

'So much of it's faded,' said Boges, 'but it looks like someone was tracing the firstborn sons down a particular branch of the Ormond family line. The Ormond Singularity seems to affect the firstborn sons.'

'You can say that again,' I muttered, thinking of the 365-day countdown, and the warning Millicent had given me about the deadly secret. 'My great-aunt,' I told Boges, 'said it had been the death of all of the Ormonds who had tried to unravel it. She said it should remain a secret.'

My friend suddenly looked nervous. We both knew that if we kept adding to the family tree, my dad's name would have been circled next, and then beneath that, mine. Would I die like my dad? That was the question I think we were both asking ourselves.

'So Ferdinand,' said Boges.

'My great-grandfather,' I added.

'Was next in line.'

'Next in line,' I said, 'to be cursed by the Ormond Singularity.'

'That's one way of looking at it. So after Ferdinand came your grandfather, and then your dad.'

'Yes,' I said. 'He was the firstborn male of that generation.'

'And then comes you. So the Ormond Singularity, whatever it is, will affect you.'

'I hope by "affect" you don't mean "kill". There have been a lot of people trying to make that happen. But the Ormond Singularity affects other people too, not just the firstborns in the family. What about that poor, crazy guy? He said the Ormond Singularity was killing him as well.'

'I think we have to remember that just *knowing* about the Ormond Singularity is dangerous.

That's why your dad warned you not to say anything.'

As Boges was laughing at a photo someone had posted on my blog—a couple of girls wearing 'Cal is innocent' T-shirts—he noticed one of the private messages from Winter.

'"Love, Little Bird"?' he asked me, reading the name she'd signed off with. 'What is that about?'

'I think her parents used to call her that,' I said. 'It's engraved on the back of her locket.'

'She's playing you like a fish on a hook.'

I thought of the last time at her flat, the way she had confided in me. 'She's given us a lot of help, Boges. Without her, we wouldn't have the Jewel, and we wouldn't have known about the writing inside it either.'

'I don't know,' said Boges, unconvinced. 'It just seems like she only offers something when you're losing faith in her. The minute it looks like you've had enough of her lies, she throws out something to draw you back in again. Look,' he said like he'd had a slight change of heart, 'I know she seems like a really cool chick, and she's helped us out a few times, but please just be careful, OK.'

I was hardly even listening to Boges because I'd just seen an oddly familiar name at the bottom of a message on my blog. It was the name that old Barty had made me repeat before he died at "Kilkenny". *The name!*

'What are you staring at? What is it?' Boges demanded, seeing the look on my face.

'Look! He's here! That's him!'

'What's there? What's him? What are you talking about?'

'The solicitor whose name I couldn't remember! That's him! Sheldrake Rathbone!'

Boges stared at the screen. Then back at me. 'Excuse me?'

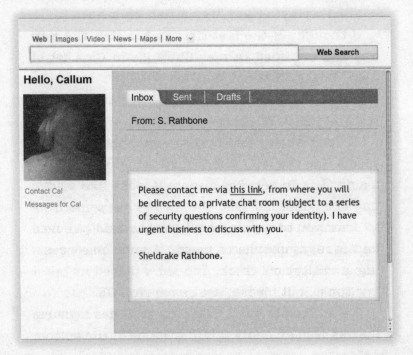

Web | Images | Video | News | Maps | More ⌄

Web Search

Hello, Callum

Contact Cal
Messages for Cal

Inbox | Sent | Drafts |

From: S. Rathbone

Please contact me via this link, from where you will be directed to a private chat room (subject to a series of security questions confirming your identity). I have urgent business to discuss with you.

Sheldrake Rathbone.

'It's him! The solicitor! The solicitor who has the Piers Ormond will!'

Boges and I stared at each other.

'Dude! What are you waiting for?'

'But what if he's a fake? And couldn't the cops hack into this?'

'I've got it all wrapped up pretty tight,' my friend assured me. 'Let's check out the security questions.'

Please answer the following security questions:

Q1: Your sister's date of birth
A1:

Q2: Your mother's maiden name
A2:

Q3: Your father's date of birth
A3:

Q4: Your father's middle name
A4:

I submitted my answers, then looked at Boges for his response when a message came up requesting a contact number.

'Don't do it,' was his answer. 'Ask for his.'

In the box I typed, 'I'd prefer to have yours, thanks.'

25 JULY

160 days to go . . .

11:14 am

I'd checked my blog, using my phone, about twenty times since Boges had left last night, anxious to see whether Sheldrake Rathbone had left a number for me to call.

When a message with his number finally showed up, I dialled right away.

'You are a hard young man to track down,' Rathbone said to me.

'I intend on it staying that way. I guess you understand I'm not living a normal sort of life right now.'

'Indeed I do. Please let me assure you of my complete discretion. It is my belief that you are innocent of the charges brought against you. You have been engaged in research concerning the Ormond Singularity?'

I was silent. I didn't know what I should admit to him, what I should give away.

'I am in possession of a certain document,'

Rathbone continued, 'which I believe will be very helpful when you combine it with the other things you may have already discovered. I acted as solicitor for some of the older members of your family. Your family has been in our firm's care for generations.'

'My Great-uncle Bartholomew told me your name,' I said. 'He said you were holding his great-uncle's will. Piers Ormond—a soldier who died in the First World War. And possibly other documents, too.'

'That is correct. Our firm holds many thousands of such documents from earlier generations. However there are certain complications that have occurred concerning this particular document.'

'Like what?' I asked, puzzled.

'A client of mine informs me that you have in your possession a valuable piece of jewellery and an old manuscript. Is this correct?'

I hesitated. How did he know that?

'How come you're so interested in me and my family?' I asked.

'It is my business to know all about the family's affairs. I have an excellent investigator who keeps me up to date with things I need to know. As well, I have private contacts, people who provide information for me. My client needs to be sure you're holding these items. She wants me to confirm it because she potentially has something of great importance for you.'

'Who is your client?'

'I'm not at liberty to tell you just yet. All in due course.'

I thought about that for a moment. I'd need to talk to Boges. The Jewel and the Riddle had cost me a lot. I didn't want to be flashing them around the place, even to a solicitor like Rathbone.

'When can we meet?' he asked.

The sound of a car pulling up outside distracted me.

'I'll call you back,' I said, before hanging up.

Car doors were slamming. I ran to the curtains—it was Boges's uncle again!

I gathered up all my stuff, shoved it in my backpack and slipped outside through the backyard. I would have to risk sneaking through the grounds of the neighbouring property.

I climbed over the ivy-covered wall that divided the mansions. Luckily, the garden of this place was like a tropical jungle and I was able to keep out of sight until I came to a problem. The bolted side gate.

I took a running jump, but the second my hand touched it, gripping the gate to help haul my body over, a deafening alarm started clanging and blue lights flashed around the house.

I charged down the side of the house, with the alarm blaring behind me.

As soon as I made it to the road I pulled out my phone to call Boges and slowed down, trying to look completely inconspicuous.

2:06 pm

Boges was wearing his sunglasses again when I met him in an alley near Liberty Mall. He apologised over and over about his uncle showing up unannounced again, but I didn't want to waste time talking about that. I needed to tell him about my conversation with Sheldrake Rathbone.

'So what do you think?' I asked. 'I don't like the idea of showing anyone the Jewel and the Riddle, but he *is* a solicitor.'

'Yeah, but I don't think you can trust anyone. Except me,' Boges added with a cheesy wink. 'Why can't he just show you the documents he has? Why do you have to show him the Riddle and the Jewel? And who the heck is his client?'

'I don't know. This whole thing is making me feel weird. Do you think he's just trying to make sure it's really *me* he's talking with?'

'What? You don't think your double, the Cal Ormond look-alike, might try to put in an appearance?'

'No,' I said, surprised by his question. 'I hadn't even thought of that. But where *does* he fit into this DMO puzzle?' I asked, suddenly distracted. 'Do I have a twin I never knew about? Bartholomew and Millicent were twins. Dad and Rafe, too . . .'

Great-aunt Millicent's strange song about the two little lambs started looping around in my head. *One was found, the other one lost.*

'Far out,' said Boges suddenly looking up from my phone. He'd been playing with it as we spoke. 'I was just having a look at your blog . . .'

'What?' I asked, snatching it from his hands.

My heart lurched when I saw the latest message that had been posted on my blog. I stared at it. For a few seconds, I couldn't believe what I was seeing.

My own mother had posted a video.

I clicked the play button.

'Cal, I know you're watching this,' she said, slowly, softly. She looked thinner, older, greyer, and was sitting at a table in Rafe's house. 'Please, darling, contact us. We are so worried about you. Gabbi's still sick. She's still in the coma . . . but we've brought her home and are looking after her here. We miss you, Cal. It has been such a long time. You know Rafe's number—all you have to do is call. I'm begging you, Cal. There is no problem we can't work out. The help you need is waiting for you. Your uncle and I are doing everything we can to find you. I love you, son. I *forgive* you. I don't care what you've done; you're my son and always will be. I don't want you to celebrate your sixteenth birthday out there on your own. Please, Cal. Please call.'

The breath was knocked out of me.

Boges looked at me with concern.

'What can I do? I know it's hard on Mum,' I said, 'but I can't just give up and go home and walk away from everything we've worked for, after everything we've been through. I won't give up on the Ormond Singularity. And I'd be going straight to a prison cell, not my old bedroom!' My head flopped into my hands. 'I can't believe she still doesn't believe me . . .'

'She will. Everyone will. One day soon,' Boges assured me. 'Madame Rodini is chasing up the translation of that inscription on the inside of the Jewel.'

'Great job of changing the subject,' I said.

4:11 pm

Boges left the Jewel and the Riddle with me once again, and I walked and walked, keeping my head down, hoping my new look would keep people off my back. I realised I'd developed a habit of constantly scanning my environment, always on the lookout. I'd heard of something called the thousand-yard stare used by soldiers whose lives depended on constantly sweeping around in three hundred and sixty degrees.

More than ever before, I wanted to see Winter. I got out my mobile to call her.

4:17 pm

'Let's meet up,' I said to her, glancing at the time. 'I know you want to see the Ormond Jewel and I'm happy to show it to you, but here's the deal.' I had to set things up in a particular way— I wanted to take charge of this meeting to ensure there were no surprises. 'You have to meet me now, and you're staying on the phone with me until I can literally see you. Until you're in my sight.'

'But Cal, I—'

'Drop whatever you're doing. It's now or never. I'm waiting at the top of the clock tower.'

'The clock tower? But—'

'Stay on the phone and start running!'

'OK, OK, I'm coming!'

The less time she had to organise anything, the better. And keeping her on the phone meant she couldn't possibly tell a soul what she was doing, and *who* she was meeting.

I could hear her rushing about, grabbing things, shutting windows, closing doors, and before long her footsteps echoed down the phone, running on concrete.

'I'm on my way,' she puffed.

'Less talk, more running.'

Within fifteen minutes, Winter Frey appeared at the top of the clock tower stairs in unbeliev- able time. She bent over, leaning on her knees, puffing and panting, hand still clutching her phone to her ear.

'You can hang up now,' I said as I walked over to her.

'Fast enough for ya?' she asked, when she looked up. Her cheeks were flushed pink, and the front strands of her hair snaked down her face. She straightened up then jumped at me, hugging me.

'Whoa, whoa,' I laughed. She'd taken me by surprise and I'd stumbled backwards, unbal- anced by her friendly pounce. I put an arm around her waist to steady us both.

'Ooh, sorry, I'm all sweaty and gross,' she said.

Again, I got that weird mixed-up feeling in my guts—happy, confused, and awkward.

'Cal, it's so good to see you again! You look so—so *straight*!'

I grinned, slowly letting her go.

'That's me. Mister Straight.'

'We should go somewhere where we can spread out,' she said, glancing around, 'and look at the Jewel safely.'

She must have seen the hesitant look on my face, and she placed a gentle hand on my arm. 'You have to trust me. I really can help. I know everything that goes on with Sligo. Well, almost everything. And now, after what's happened with Zombrovski . . . What *did* happen with Zombrovski? No, save that gory story for later. If Sligo ever suspected that I was helping you . . .' The blood drained out of Winter's face and for a moment she looked like a scared little kid. The part of me that didn't quite trust her was quickly absorbed by all the parts that did.

'Hey,' I said, touching her hand. 'It's OK. He's never going to find out—not from me.'

I should have taken my hand away then, but I couldn't. It was like there was a charge running between us.

She slowly pulled her hand away. 'Sligo's away at the moment so my place is safer than ever. Let's go there?'

'You're joking.' I remembered last time, and Sligo coming up the fire-escape.

'Believe me, he's out of town. One of his top guys was taken *out*,' she said with a knowing look, 'and his other guy was taken *in*, so Sligo's out recruiting more help. Replacements. My place will be cool, I promise. Cross my heart and hope to die,' she said, marking an invisible cross on her chest.

No doubt Sligo was scrambling to clean up the mess after Zombrovski plunged to his death, and Bruno—was he behind bars? Was that what she meant?

12 Lesley Street

5:25 pm

We were at Winter's tiny place, on the roof of the old apartment building. She grabbed some cans of soft drink out of her fridge and put them on the counter, along with a packet of pretzels, while I started pulling things out of my bag. Music from a small radio played softly in the background.

Winter took out a little notebook, then sat down, waiting expectantly.

I went to her front door and locked it. I looked out the front windows, past the geraniums, and the empty clothesline, then closed her curtains. I was aware she was watching my every move.

When I sat back down, we went over everything that had gone on since we'd last spoken, and I explained in detail what had happened to Zombie. She listened, intrigued, munching on pretzels and nodding. She said Sligo was furious when he found out, even punched a hole in one of the doors at his new place.

'I have some really old letters written by Piers Ormond,' I said. 'He mentions an amazing story he heard about our family.' I paused. 'That's exactly what Dad said in his letter. Isn't it weird, how it's happening again, nearly a hundred years later?'

'History often repeats itself,' she said before leaning towards me. 'You looked really sad then, when you mentioned your dad.'

I nodded. 'It's the anniversary of his death tomorrow. I've kind of been dreading it.'

I had to turn away from her face because if I'd kept looking at the concern in her eyes, I'd have started crying. Very uncool. I cleared my throat and continued. 'Piers Ormond was gathering important information. He left his findings with the family solicitor for safekeeping nearly one hundred years ago. But then he died in the First World War and never reclaimed the documents. So whatever the secret was, it stayed locked up in some solicitor's filing system and nothing more was done about it—until my dad stumbled onto something last year at the conference in Ireland.'

'Your dad picked up where Piers stopped,' she said. 'And now you've picked it up for both of them.'

'Right. We thought Dad had gone crazy and wasted all our savings because his brain was so messed up, but it wasn't that at all. Somehow, he must have tracked down the Jewel—found out that it still existed in one piece, then spent the money buying it back.'

'Well? Where is this famous Ormond Jewel? Let me see it already! The suspense is killing me!' she smiled.

I laid the Jewel on the table.

'Oh my,' she gasped, picking it up. 'I have never seen anything so beautiful! I can't imagine how much money something like this must be worth.' She turned it over in her hands. 'Not just for the jewels—that huge emerald and the pearls and rubies—but for the fact that it's hundreds of years old.'

She carefully opened it and gazed at the portrait in its oval frame. 'And look, there's the inscription that I told you about,' she said tracing the line of tiny engraved letters with her fingertip.

'This is what it says,' I said, pulling out the piece of paper on which Boges had written the foreign words.

'Amor et suevre tosjors celer,' she quoted, with what I guessed was a perfect French accent. 'Just imagine how much this Elizabethan miniature portrait alone is worth,' she said. 'Cal, you can't just be carrying this thing around in a backpack! This is a priceless antique. You need to put it somewhere safe. At least in a box or something.'

'I gave it to Boges to look after while I went to see my great-aunt, but now it's back with me and I sleep with it by my side. It's always with me. It can't get safer than that.'

Winter turned her attention to the Ormond Riddle and read it again with great concentration. She looked pretty awesome with her wild hair and its glittering ribbons framing her serious face as she worked. For a few minutes, as she studied first the Riddle and then the Jewel, I studied her, remembering the last time I'd been here and how close we'd seemed—two outsiders who didn't belong anywhere—who no longer had a family they could turn to.

Suddenly, she jumped up, holding the Ormond Riddle, her hands shaking with excitement, her eyes huge with surprise.

Her mouth opened as if she were about to speak, then closed again. 'Oh my God!'

'What is it?'

'I've just seen something!'

'*What?*'

Ribbons sparkled as the infuriating girl shook her head.

'First you have to tell me everything you know about this amazing jewel, and then I'll tell you what I've just noticed. I can't believe no-one else has picked this up before!'

Her eyes were shining with excitement, but her mouth was very determined.

'So tell me then. You tell me what you can see,' I said, trying like crazy to see what she had just seen.

Winter Frey stood there, drumming the fingers of her folded arms, waiting. Then she firmly shook her head. 'No way. You first. I need to know that you've told me everything before I say any more.'

'Why are you making this so hard?' I said. 'Just tell me what I need to know without all this *drama*.'

'This is *not* drama!' she cried, her eyebrows gathering together in a frown. 'The more you tell me, the easier it will be to solve this! You guys need all the help you can get! You and your friend haven't been able to work out what I've just seen. I have the sort of mind that is good with mysteries. I've been living with mysteries most of my life!'

'Living with mysteries? What do you mean?'

'Never mind,' she said.

'OK,' I relented. 'You pretty much already know everything I know. How my great-uncle read out a description of the Jewel to me, and how it fits with this,' I pointed to the glowing jewel lying in front of us. 'And how these two pieces, the Riddle and the Jewel, go together to solve the mystery of the Ormond Singularity. That they form—'

'The two halves of the double-key code,' she interrupted, like she was trying to rush my words out for me.

'Right.'

'Your great-uncle was spot on!'

'What have you just seen?' I repeated, running out of patience.

I watched her looking excitedly at the Jewel and then back to the Riddle. She picked up the Jewel and held it reverently in her hand, gently opening it. 'I guess you know who *she* is?'

'Sure I do. Queen Elizabeth the First. She gave the Jewel to one of my ancestors.'

She gave me a triumphant glance. 'So what else do you know about this ancestor?'

'He was Black Tom Butler, the tenth Earl of Ormond. He and his family acted as the Queen's stewards, working in the interests of the Crown. It was a tricky job. Trying to keep in the good books with his Irish countrymen as well as staying popular with the Queen. But he must have done well because she gave him this. Remember, we worked out ages ago that the drawing of the waiter pointed to the word "butler", and if you look at the drawing of the boy with the rose, you'll see that there's a rose on the back of the Jewel.'

Winter turned the Jewel over once more, at the same time glancing across to the drawings, looking from one to the next.

'Come on. Quit stalling. If you really know something, spit it out.'

'Just a couple more questions, promise. I get that your dad drew this Sphinx to tell you about the Riddle, but what's with the head of Caesar? Any ideas about that?'

'No. Nothing so far. Except that it could mean something about a great ruler, or leader. The Queen, maybe. We don't have anything on the monkey either.'

'Great.'

She wasn't being sarcastic. I looked at her in surprise.

'What's great about it?'

'I like a challenge,' she purred. 'The trickier the better. I'll chase up everything I can on Caesar and riddles and pyramids and sphinxes. I'll check out monkeys with jewelled collars and golden balls. I think I said once before that he looked familiar.'

She made a note for herself.

'Maybe it's somebody's pet?' she suggested. 'It has that cute collar. Maybe your dad couldn't draw the person he really meant to tell you about, so he drew the person's pet?'

It was as good a suggestion as anything I could think of. 'It's possible,' I said. 'That's how my dad's brain was functioning towards the end.'

'You look really sad again. You OK?'

I nodded. Although it made me feel a bit better when she noticed, it also made it harder. Her concern forced me to deal with how I was feeling, and most of the time I just wanted to push it all away. Far, far away.

'Like I said before, tomorrow is his anniversary,' I said. 'I can't believe it's been a year. There are so many questions I want to ask him. And things I'd like to say. But that's not possible and it's like this big, shadowy tombstone looming up in the middle of the year, days before my birthday. I just need to get past it.'

She didn't say anything and I was relieved. Again, I had the sense that Winter really knew what I was going through.

'Also, right now,' I continued, 'I need to be totally focused on solving this,' I looked at everything on the table, 'and whatever it is that you've just seen. If you're ever going to tell me.'

She nodded. 'OK, last thing,' she said, sliding the transparency closer with the tip of her little finger. 'Please tell me what you know about this.'

'One of the words is the name of a place in Ireland—maybe where Dad stayed or something. Not sure about the other one.'

'I can tell you this for free,' she said. 'Vulkan is determined to discover what the Ormond Singularity is, and he will try anything to make sure nobody gets there before he does. You must be very careful, Cal. He wants that Jewel back desperately, and he has it in for you more than ever now that he's lost a man.'

'He's not the only one who has it in for me. He'll have to join the queue.'

'OK,' she said, her eyes sparkling with energy. 'I'll tell you what I've seen in this double-key code.' She picked up her own, handwritten copy of the Riddle as she spoke. 'I've been obsessing over this. I've learned it off by heart. These words have almost become a part of me, and the minute I opened up the Jewel and saw the Queen's portrait inside, I had a sudden flash: I thought—what if the lady mentioned in the Riddle is Queen Elizabeth? The same as in the Jewel?'

A light flashed on in my brain. 'So,' I said thinking aloud, 'if that lady in the Riddle is this lady inside the Jewel, then those words about leaves and grace and numbers and all the other stuff—are describing this locket with her portrait inside?'

Winter's vigorous nodding was infectious. 'You got it,' she said. 'That's exactly it! When I saw the Jewel I immediately noticed a couple of things.'

Her face, usually pale, was lit up with colour. With her glowing cheeks, she suddenly looked like just an ordinary girl—instead of Winter Frey.

'You know how I thought it might have been a number riddle?' she continued. 'Cal, how many of those gold leaves are there surrounding the emerald?'

I peered closer and counted them.

'Eight.'

'*Eight are the leaves on my Ladyes Grace,*' Winter recited. 'Eight!'

I checked the Jewel, counting carefully. There was no doubt about it. There were eight small golden leaves winding around the outside of the emerald, four on each side. Eight leaves in the Ormond Riddle, eight leaves on the Ormond Jewel.

'But what's the *Ladyes Grace*?'

'The Ormond Jewel is the Queen's gift—her "grace" to Black Tom. Think about it. She graced your family with this beautiful gift.'

Something electric surged through my body.

Winter was amazing! My mind was racing, trying to see more and more of the connections between the piece of vellum and the glowing jewel.

Winter's words tumbled out in excitement. 'Don't you see? This line describes the Queen's portrait in its oval frame: *Fayre sits the rounde of my Ladyes face.*'

She looked up at me, her face shining. 'I've been studying *Henry V* with my tutor Miss Sparks. She said that if you change the Shakespearean English into modern language, that line would go something like, "the portrait of my lady's face sits nicely in its frame".'

'You've told your tutor about this riddle?'

'No way!' she laughed. 'I just told her I was reading some Shakespearean poetry. She was so excited that I was showing an interest! She helped me with the language. She told me that funny-looking word in the last line—*yifte*—is actually *gift*. She explained how sometimes copyists wrote "g" without quite closing up the top of the letter, so that it got mistaken for a "y". But then she got real interested in what poem I was reading and I had to change the subject fast.'

I looked at the pearls and rubies that ran around the oval emerald, between it and the eight leaves. On a hunch, I started counting the rubies. There were sixteen. That didn't match up with anything. But when I counted the pearls a flash of excitement moved me. I counted them again.

'Winter! There are thirteen of them! Thirteen pearls!'

'The thirteen tears!' she said. 'The Riddle says thirteen tears!' Her eyes widened again. 'Of course! That's it! That's what pearls were called in the olden days! Tears of the moon! Thirteen tears!'

I looked at the Ormond Jewel more closely.

Thirteen tears. Thirteen pearls.

'Wow,' I whispered.

The two halves of the double-key code were really coming together. I thought about Boges and how pumped he would be with this new breakthrough. Pumped enough not to give me too hard a time over meeting up with Winter again, I hoped. The Riddle was throwing light on the Jewel—secretly describing it. We were getting closer.

'What are you doing?' I asked Winter. She was hunched over her open notebook, sketching something.

'Drawing it,' she said, looking up at me with a grin. 'Is that OK? Having a picture of the Jewel means I can keep working on the puzzle.'

'Good idea,' I said, happy to be making progress.

I watched as Winter deftly drew the outline of the Jewel, with the eight leaves and thirteen pearls clearly defined around the massive emerald.

Realising with a start that we'd been talking for a long time, I began gathering everything up, thinking I should go. Winter stopped what she was doing and watched as I repacked my backpack.

'I should go,' I said, kind of like a question, more than a statement.

'Cal,' she said, moving closer to me and looking into my eyes with such intensity it almost made me uneasy. I stopped shoving things into my backpack.

'I've found a way,' she said softly, 'to ask my parents things, to talk to them.'

I stared at her. 'What do you mean?'

'I don't mean all that psychic stuff, just something really simple that seems to work for me. I know that love is eternal—it's part of our soul. And even though my mum and dad aren't here with me any more, I can still talk to them. And you know what? The best thing is that answers *do* come. When I have something on my mind, I go to them. I go to the cemetery and sit near their graves. It might sound a bit spooky, but it's really not. It's actually quite peaceful. Often I'm sitting there and the answers just come to me, float into my mind.'

I frowned, considering what she'd just said. 'So you think if I went to where Dad . . .'

'I'm sure of it. It's been a year since you lost your dad. I'll come with you. It always helps to have a friend who understands.'

That last phrase made me smile. *A friend who understands.*

'Tonight? On the eve?' I asked.

Winter nodded.

'I don't think we'll be able to get inside the vault,' I said. 'Dad's in a mausoleum,' I explained.

'That's doesn't matter. Cool, let's do it.'

Crookwood Cemetery
First Avenue, Crookwood

11:25 pm

Winter and I hurried past the stone wall of the cemetery, heading towards the main gates. I knew they'd be locked at this hour, almost midnight, but the darkness of the night gave us the best cover for climbing over and getting in.

We made our way past the silent graves and brooding vaults. The white, marble figures of angels and columns looked grey in the dim starlight and the light breeze chilled our faces and rustled the leaves in the surrounding trees. I made my way easily and quickly through the winding paths with Winter close beside me.

'Here it is,' I whispered when we reached the Ormond vault. My gaze fell on the lock on the door—to my surprise it looked the same as it had when I'd last been here, in January. I had assumed Rafe would have changed the lock after the drawings went missing from the storage container he'd hidden inside.

I put my bag down and started fumbling around inside, checking to see whether I still had the old key on my chain. When my fingers found it I slipped it out and into the lock. It fitted perfectly. With a deft tweak and a bit of a push, the heavy door gave way, creaking as it opened.

'Come on,' I said to Winter. 'I'll switch my torch on once we're inside and I've closed the door again.'

Winter took my hand and stepped briskly in behind me. We closed the door and I flicked on my torch. Immediately, the dusty interior of the mausoleum came into view, with the caskets on the benches, and the remains of withered flowers and wreaths. I flashed the light around. Rafe's storage boxes were no longer there.

Winter released her grip on my hand and grabbed something from a pocket in her skirt. When she opened her hand, I saw that she had brought with her three half-burned tea-light candles and some matches. I watched as she stood them in a row along a shelf, then lit them.

She smiled in the soft, solemn glow. 'What's down there?' she asked, pointing to the stone steps leading down into more darkness.

'Some very old Ormonds.'

'I'm glad I wore my coat,' she said with a shiver. 'It's cold in here. Cold, but peaceful.'

She was right. The last time I'd been here, to find the envelope with the drawings, I had been with Boges who was spooked, thinking of ghouls, but tonight with Winter it was different. We sat down, cross-legged on the floor.

'What would you say to your dad?' she asked. 'If he were here?'

I gazed at the dusty lid of the urn that held my dad's ashes, unsure of how to answer. 'I guess I'd tell him I miss him,' I said, finally. 'And that I'm doing everything I can to finish what he started. Stay alive, solve this mystery and put our family back together.'

'He'd be so proud of you, Cal.'

I looked up at Winter. 'What do you say to your parents?'

I was taken aback—she had tears in her eyes. She wiped her face with the back of her hand.

'At first,' she said, looking down and fiddling with her skirt, 'I told them how bad I felt about the car accident. About how I felt like it was all my fault.' She stopped to look up at me. 'I haven't told you exactly what happened to my parents . . . It was my tenth birthday when it happened. It was my birthday,' she repeated, 'and I wanted to go to the aquarium to see the seahorses. Mum and Dad both seemed really stressed and busy, but I chucked a bit of a tantrum and made them take me.'

She stopped and took a deep breath before continuing.

'On our way there, driving down a bend on this steep, winding road we'd travelled along a thousand times, Dad lost control of the car. I know I was mucking around and I probably distracted him, but I remember the car skidding sideways, and Dad grabbing hopelessly at the wheel, his eyes in the rear-view mirror frantic, trying to protect his family. I saw Mum reach for his knee, then the car rolled and my whole world tumbled upside-down. I'd undone my seatbelt earlier—a habit they were always getting mad at me for—so when we started crashing down the side of the road, I was flung out. I landed in a bushy flat, with barely a scratch on me. But the car, with my parents trapped helplessly inside, kept on rolling and crashed on the rocks way below the road.' Winter looked deep into my eyes again. She looked so sad, exposed, vulnerable. 'They didn't have a chance.'

She took another deep breath, the only sound in that deep stillness. It seemed that even the spirits of the dead were listening to her words with rapt attention.

'I blamed myself. Sometimes I still do, but I've learned a lot in the last few years and I've come to realise that you can't control everything that happens in your life. I know I didn't cause that accident. Bad weather, a slippery road and worn brakes maybe, but not me.'

I silently nodded, letting her keep talking.

'But now I want to find that car. I need to see it. You know how you thought ages ago that you saw me at Sligo's car yard, prowling around? Looking under tarpaulins?'

'Yeah?' I asked, curiously, wondering where this was headed.

'I'm sorry I never admitted it to you before, but it *was* me. I lied to you. I hated doing that. But I just wasn't ready to tell you—or tell anybody really—about what I was there for, and why it's important I find it, see the damage, and then let it go.'

'But the car would have been destroyed ages ago,' I said.

'Possibly,' she said. 'But I just have this feeling it's in Sligo's car yard. Piled up somewhere among all the other car bodies. I feel it more than ever when I'm near my parents' graves. It's like they're trying to tell me something . . .'

The candles flickered and dimmed, then flared up again as the wind blew through a crack near the mausoleum door.

26 JULY

159 days to go . . .

12:02 am

'You know,' Winter said, looking around, 'you could make a good little hideout here. You have privacy upstairs and downstairs, a good lock on the door, plus I'm pretty sure your neighbours wouldn't make any noise,' she said with a giggle.

The candles had burned down pretty low. Winter leaned over one and dipped her finger in the melting wax. 'It's after midnight,' she announced as she examined her fingertip.

'We'd better go,' I said. 'But I feel like I should leave something behind, something that shows I was here, on Dad's anniversary.'

I dug around in my backpack and was about to give up when something pricked my finger. I pulled it out. It was the guardian angel pin that Repro had given me. Gently, I laid it on top of Dad's urn, where it glinted softly.

'Miss you, Dad,' I whispered. 'Here's an angel to watch over you.'

30 JULY

155 days to go . . .

S Enid Parade, Crystal Beach

11:49 am

My mobile vibrated in my pocket.

📱 check your blog. very interesting development.

I did as Boges suggested and logged onto my blog. When I saw the initials at the bottom of the private message I'd received, I almost fell over.

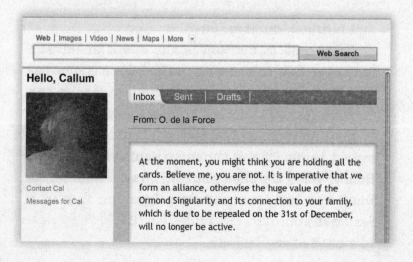

Web | Images | Video | News | Maps | More ▾

[   ] **Web Search**

Hello, Callum

Contact Cal
Messages for Cal

Inbox   Sent   Drafts

From: O. de la Force

At the moment, you might think you are holding all the cards. Believe me, you are not. It is imperative that we form an alliance, otherwise the huge value of the Ormond Singularity and its connection to your family, which is due to be repealed on the 31st of December, will no longer be active.

All will be lost, forever. Or even worse, Vulkan Sligo, who is well advanced in unravelling the meaning, will win through and gain what should rightly be yours.

I recognise that you have no reason to trust me and that is why I am suggesting the first of two appointments. The first is a goodwill gesture and requires only that you prove to Sheldrake Rathbone (who has agreed to act as my legal intermediary) that you do indeed have the Ormond Riddle and the Ormond Jewel in your possession. In return, he will give you a copy of the Piers Ormond will, and information concerning a more personal mystery in your own life—one that is related to the abduction of twin boys some 15 years ago.

In the second meeting, we can talk, and work out a way of moving forward with this together.

I feel sure you will agree to these meetings which are in your interests as well as mine. Please call Sheldrake Rathbone as soon as possible.

O.F.

I blinked, dumbfounded.

Oriana de la Force was the client Sheldrake Rathbone had referred to in his phone conversation with me! She was using the services of the Ormond family solicitor! The man with the Piers Ormond will! And yet she'd admitted that whatever benefit the Ormond Singularity brought with it when decoded should rightly be mine. So what was in it for her? Now my mind was in a real mess.

I needed my friends.

12 Lesley Street

2:00 pm

Winter and Boges sat beside me at the table, deep concern and suspicion in both of their faces. I was relieved Boges had agreed to join us at Winter's flat. He'd been pretty impressed with the double-key code connections Winter and I had figured out, and we were all keen to kick on and sort the DMO out.

'What are you going to do?' Winter asked. 'Do you think you can trust anything Oriana de la Force says after everything that's happened?'

I was incredulous. 'She's almost had me killed more times than I can count! She's had me kidnapped, bugged, followed, beaten . . . Her thugs are the reason my great-uncle is dead!'

My mind was seething with questions. Did Oriana de la Force really think that we could be *allies*? She was offering me information I desperately needed—whatever was contained in the Piers Ormond will was something I absolutely had to know.

And, above all, I was astounded by her claim that she knew something about the abduction of the twin babies, fifteen years ago . . . fifteen years! What did that mean for me? Was I really a twin? Could I really have a long-lost brother?

So many questions, so many doubts, so many fears swirled through my mind. Things had been much simpler when Oriana de la Force was just an enemy.

'You OK?' asked Winter.

I shook my head.

'And what about this Rathbone guy?' Boges's voice penetrated my spinning thoughts. 'Can we trust him?'

'Sheldrake Rathbone is the Ormond family solicitor,' I said, trying to shake my senses back into me. 'The man holding Piers Ormond's will. Says he believes I'm innocent.'

'So? What are you going to do?' Winter repeated.

'Not sure.'

Who am I? I asked myself. Had my whole life, my whole identity, been based on lies and cover-ups? This twin stuff had my mind reeling more than anything else. It was like everybody, including my own parents, was harbouring this massive, dark secret about me, and no-one wanted to fess up and explain it to me . . . except Oriana. Whatever the truth was, *I* needed to know.

'I guess there's no harm in just calling him,' I said, as I pulled out my mobile and dialled Rathbone's number. I flicked the loudspeaker function on.

2:12 pm

'I've been expecting your call,' said Rathbone. 'I have agreed to act as intermediary on behalf of a colleague. You know her?'

'I know her,' I admitted, grimly.

'I believe she has already made it clear that she wishes to negotiate with you following an initial meeting between us to confirm you have certain items in your possession. Once I've satisfied myself that this is the case, I will be happy to provide you with information regarding the crime involving the twin babies that I think you would appreciate knowing about, as well as hand over a copy of a will that I believe is of great interest to you.'

'Shouldn't I have free access to that information without all this show and tell and exchange?' I asked. 'It's a family matter—*my* family matter.'

The sound of his low, wheezy chuckle reverberated around Winter's flat. It was the kind of laugh that made me picture him as a big guy that didn't think things were funny very often. I looked at Winter and Boges, and they were both cringing.

'Now, Cal, can you really expect me to hand over a valuable family document to someone in your situation? Someone on the run? Someone accused of murder, without anything in return?

Shouldn't you be more concerned that I might hand you over to the police and claim the reward money the minute you show up?' He chuckled again, deep and loud, and it bothered me. There was nothing funny about what he was saying.

'How do I know you won't do that?' I demanded.

'Look, my role in this is to act purely as an intermediary, and to provide a neutral place where I can review the objects in your keeping in a safe and satisfactory manner. I'm not interested in money—I have enough of that already,' he scoffed. 'And I'm certainly not interested in handing you in and getting involved with that side of law enforcement. I have a place in mind for our meeting—the premises of my brother's business, Rathbone, Greaves and Diggory. This arrangement between us needs to be finalised within the next forty-eight hours, or my client will withdraw her offer. Do you understand?'

'So what's the deal?' I asked.

'You need to be at the premises tomorrow, after business hours. Say eight o'clock. 317 Temperance Lane. It runs off Mason Place. Do you know it?'

Winter was nodding at me, telling me she knew it.

'I can work it out,' I said. 'I'll be there.'

'With the required items,' Sheldrake reminded

me. 'There is a rear lane entrance which will be left unlocked for you. Go straight in. There'll be an envelope with your name on it waiting for you, containing the information you require. Once I arrive and see for myself that you're in possession of the items in question, we can go our separate ways. After that point you will wait for me to call with further instructions on the second appointment involving Ms de la Force. Is that understood?'

'See you there.'

2:23 pm

'I'm going with you,' said Boges.

'Me too,' added Winter. 'There's no way you can go on your own. Who knows what they have planned.'

'We could get there early and run a security sweep of the area,' said Boges, 'and then wait for you in hiding, just outside.'

'We'll both be watching your back,' said Winter. 'If you're sure you want to do this?'

'I'm sure,' I said, feeling completely the opposite. I couldn't imagine ever having Oriana de la Force as an ally. Not in a billion years. I figured I'd go to the first meeting with Rathbone, get the envelope, then get out of there. I would never agree to a meeting with Oriana.

'Tomorrow night you might find out the truth about your double,' said Boges. 'I hope you're ready for it.'

31 JULY

154 days to go . . .

12:00 am

📱 cal, it's winter. just wanted to be the first in with a 'HAPPY BIRTHDAY!' xo

10:13 am

📱 happy birthday cal. let's hope tonight brings u some answers. c u later. boges.

Temperance Lane

7:45 pm

The three of us had spent an hour crouched in an alley, discreetly checking out 317 Temperance Lane. It was on a narrow winding street that led off Mason Place just as Rathbone had described.

In my backpack was the text of the Ormond Riddle and the Ormond Jewel. The three of us stood up. I knew it would be impossible to secure such a place but with Boges and Winter offering to keep a lookout at each end of the lane while I went in, I hoped everything would be OK.

'I'll wait here,' said Boges when we reached the corner of the lane, 'and keep watch. If anyone who looks like trouble arrives, I'll let you know.' He pulled out his mobile.

'I'll do the same at the other end of the lane,' said Winter. 'Are you sure you don't want one of us to go in with you?'

I shook my head. 'I can handle this. Any sign of something out of order, and I'll be out of there like a rocket.'

'And don't be long,' said Winter. 'We have a birthday to celebrate when you get out!'

7:57 pm

I approached the shopfront cautiously. In the streetlight, I could just make out that the gate at the rear entrance to Rathbone, Greaves and Diggory was slightly ajar. I pushed it open, and stepped inside.

Everything was very quiet. I was on red alert. But the building seemed as quiet as the Ormond mausoleum. Deserted.

Sheldrake Rathbone would be here any moment, I thought, glancing at my watch. I wondered about the information waiting for me as I trod stealthily down the short hallway to what looked like a larger room at the end of it. Although the lights were out, a streetlight shone in through the windows. I stood there for a few moments, puzzled by what I saw. Then I realised what kind of business I was standing in.

Sheldrake Rathbone's brother was an undertaker! Rathbone, Greaves and Diggory was a funeral parlour!

Coffins and caskets in light and dark timbers, silver handles glinting, were displayed on trestles, some of them gaping open to reveal the satin lining inside the polished wood. Some were barely finished, awaiting the final trim of fabric. A white one was lavishly painted inside like the Sistine Chapel, with cloudy skies and cherubs all over it.

Around the walls, and stacked behind the counter, several coffins were stored standing upright. A small room off to the left of them seemed to be the workroom, its floor covered with corkscrews of shaved timber.

I looked around for the envelope that Rathbone had said would be there for me. My eyes locked onto it, sitting alone on the counter.

Near the doorway to the workroom, beside a large black coffin standing against the wall, was a list of the burials for the next day. There was only one down for that day, I noticed. I leaned forward to try and read the name. As I did, I caught a whiff of a faint scent that I recognised but couldn't quite place; something familiar.

An unusual sound followed.

I swung around. 'Who's there?' I called.

Silence again. I wondered if I should get out, go back to the street and call Rathbone.

I wasn't leaving without the envelope. I reached out to pick it up and bang! The counter suddenly flew open, slamming into my face, hitting me square on the forehead.

It wasn't a counter! It was a coffin! And something had flung the lid open and was leaping out at me!

Shocked and disoriented, I stumbled backwards, reeling from the blow to my forehead. I held my hand up, trying to protect myself against the charging figure from inside the coffin.

I barely noticed his cowboy-style shoes as he came down on top of me. I kicked and punched, staggering backwards. A sharp jab stung my neck. I grabbed at it, twisting and turning to try and see my attacker.

Something weird was happening to me. A burning sensation started spreading over my shoulders and up into my face. I kept trying to turn around, but I was in slow motion, like in a nightmare, barely able to move. I felt my backpack being wrenched from my shoulders. My vision rippled like a mirage as I saw a dark figure shove my backpack into the casket painted like the Sistine Chapel.

My rippling vision turned into a haze, then faded to black. I kept fighting to keep my mind alive, but it was impossible. I couldn't stop the darkness . . .

11:01 pm

I couldn't move. I blinked my eyes a few times, but everything was still black. The stinging sensation from earlier had changed into a complete numbness that had taken over my whole body.

It was pitch black and I sensed something very close to my face. Using every ounce of willpower, I tried to force my fingers to move, but they wouldn't! I couldn't move! A strange sense of claustrophobia came over me and I felt hemmed in on every side, top and bottom as well, like I'd been wedged into some sort of confined crawl space.

What was going on? Where was I? I had to get out and find my backpack!

Suddenly I was jolted as if being lifted by unseen hands. Was this some weird effect of whatever stupefying drug I'd been given? The jolting continued until I heard a scraping noise and was pushed forward. My head shifted a little and that's when my nose touched something soft and very close to me. That's when the full horror of my position was revealed.

I was sealed up in something. A box of some sort. *I was trapped inside a coffin, being loaded into a hearse!*

I tried to scream, but was unable to control my mouth. Nothing happened. I tried to struggle, but I still couldn't move. With another sudden jolt, the vehicle I'd been loaded into started to move. I remembered the burial list on the wall of the undertakers. There had been one name on it.

My name!

Again, I tried to scream but it was no use.

The box vibrated as the hearse began to drive. Was I being driven to a *cemetery*?

On and on, the drive continued. I was petrified—hopelessly numb. I kept trying to move my fingers and my toes.

I suddenly became very aware of my breathing. How much air was in this coffin?

Even in my drowsy state, I understood that it wouldn't matter how much air was trapped inside here with me. Within a very short time, six feet underground, I would be dead.

I had failed to survive my sixteenth birthday.

11:38 pm

The sounds of the car engine stopped and I could hear voices outside, muffled by the padding in the coffin. I wanted to scream and yell and shout, and bang the walls around me, but my hands and mouth still wouldn't work.

Great-aunt Millicent's haunting words, explaining how she knew my dad was dead, seeped into my mind.

'*Because anyone who starts to investigate the Ormond Singularity . . . winds up in a casket . . .*'

Through the tangled, gluey muddle in my mind, my panic grew out of control. I visualised everything that was happening to me. With a sickening jerk, I felt myself being dragged across the ground then lowered. Slowly, slowly the coffin shuddered . . . until I hit the bottom of a grave.

Thud.

The first shovelful of dirt hit the coffin lid on top of me.

Thud.

The second. This can't be happening!

Thud.

The third. And then the dirt started falling faster, heavier . . .

Thud, thud, thud . . .

CONSPIRACY 365

BOOK EIGHT: AUGUST

'What has happened to Gabbi? Has she been kidnapped?' I screamed at him. 'Tell me what has happened to my sister!'

Cal's worst nightmare has come true – his sister is still in a coma, but now she's been kidnapped by his enemies and is being held ransom. He's got to get out of the secure wing of the hospital where he's being held, but nobody believes the 'psycho kid' and he's running out of people he can trust. He's going to need all the help Winter and Boges can give him to win the race for Gabbi's life . . .